FLOWER & CLOAK

First edition. January 31, 2022.

Copyright © 2022 Stephanie Ascough.

ISBN: 978-1734981223

Written by Stephanie Ascough.

Table of Contents

To the Flower Hearts, in every season.

Little Red

"You're sure it went that way?" the wolf said.

Little Red nodded, her wide eyes taking in the lip-curling snarl, the sharp yellow teeth, and the hairy medium frame. This one was hungry, not starving.

"And it was a big one, you say?"

The girl didn't move as the creature circled her. "The biggest I've ever seen," she answered.

The wolf's lips twisted into a grimace. "You're lucky," he said. "I'd rather not floss my teeth with your clothes today. And I've always liked fast food."

Little Red watched the wolf bound away and released a frosted puff of breath. She grinned. That one had been easy to fool. Fooling was better than killing, but she could kill when necessary. Little Red was no stranger to wolves of all kinds.

She shifted the heavy basket on her arm–carefully, so as to not crush the cakes–and went on her way, her crimson cape swirling around her. Now it was time for something much more pleasant. Visiting her granny in the woods was always an adventure, but she always made it there in one piece.

Soon, her favorite cottage came into view, peeking through gold and scarlet leaves. She was proud to be named after Granny, after the color they both loved. Granny had sewn two little hearts, one within the other, on the lining of her velvet cape. "One for me, one for you," Granny had told her, giving her a smile and a hug.

Little Red fingered those hearts as she reached the door. She paused, her hand on the doorknob, when an unfamiliar voice sounded from behind the door. Someone strange was in Granny's house. Her mother had always taught her to be polite, so she knocked, just in case she was interrupting something. But why would Granny have company when she had invited Little Red?

At her knock, Granny's voice called, "Who is it?"

"It's me, Little Red," she answered.

"Come in." The familiar, warm voice sounded different, almost relieved. Something was definitely wrong.

Little Red pushed open the door to see her beloved granny, white with fear, facing a hooded stranger who stood with their back to the door. Red hot anger boiled inside the girl. No one threatened her granny without regretting it. Before she could move, the stranger turned and the hood fell back, revealing a severe-looking woman who eyed Little Red with equal parts astonishment and wariness. Light blonde hair framed her face. She looked both old and young, as if she'd been caught between years for so long that her features couldn't decide how old she was anymore.

"So," said the stranger, "you've been busy, eh, Red?"

It took the girl a second to understand that this stranger wasn't speaking to her.

"Yes. This is my granddaughter." Granny walked over to her and put her gnarled hands on her shoulders, silencing Little Red's questions with a squeeze.

"This doesn't change anything." The woman crossed her arms. "I've been looking for you for a long time."

"I have a family to look after now," said Granny, her sweet, old lady's voice edged with defiance. Her hands gripped the girl's shoulders a little too tightly so that she almost winced. "I've changed, Alice."

Little Red blinked, confused. No one ever evoked this sort of response in her granny, this kind of desperation. Who was this Alice? An even more uncomfortable question crept into her mind: who was her Granny, really? She always thought she'd known. Now doubt loomed before her in the shape of this young-old intruder.

"The rules of Wonderland don't change." Alice pulled a scroll out from her cloak and handed it to Granny, who looked at it as though it was a wolf about to bite her.

Little Red caught the words "Notice of Trial" written on it.

"You've evaded the law for fifty years—give or take a few."

"I left to start a new life," said Grandmother softly.

"You were a queen, and a terrible one at that." Alice crossed her arms. "You were supposed to be tried for your crimes. Instead, you escaped."

"Please, Alice. If I leave my family, they'll worry for me. Wonderland time isn't like forest time. Do you want an old lady to come back to find all her family gone, or grown so old they've forgotten her?" Granny was actually pleading, her hands clasped together. The scroll lay discarded on the floor.

Little Red was horrified. *I'd never forget you,* she thought. And *no one* made her granny beg.

Alice's jaw worked. "I'll give you twenty-four hours to tell your family what you've got to do," she said. "Then if you don't come for the trial, I'll send the Jabberwocky to bring you."

"What if I kill your Jabberwocky?" Little Red demanded.

The words rang in her own ears. She wasn't sure she'd meant to say them out loud. Alice looked at her as if seeing an oddity for the first time–which couldn't be, if she knew of something as outrageous as a Jabberwocky. Little Red had no idea what it was, but with such a ridiculous name, how bad could it be?

She waved away the start of Granny's protests. "I'm old enough to defend myself," she said. "Why shouldn't I defend you?"

"Rules are rules," Alice said. "Your granny has to answer for her crimes. If she comes quietly, all the better."

"What if she's found guilty?" Little Red said.

A sneer crossed the cloaked woman's face. "Then let justice be done."

Little Red's mind spun. She didn't think Granny would survive Alice's notions of justice. The woman had tracked her across worlds and years, determined to make the former queen pay for a past that both women saw differently.

But Little Red had outwitted smart wolves and killed fierce ones. Wolves were a lot like people. The only difference was what they wanted.

"How about this?" Little Red set down her basket and drew herself up to her full height, crossing her arms over her chest. The cloaked woman raised an eyebrow in bored mockery. "If my granny is found guilty, I'll challenge the Jabberwocky to a fight."

Alice scoffed, but Granny's voice spoke, full of pride. "Little Red has killed wolves before," she said. She sounded like herself again. "I wouldn't refuse if I were you. The child is my heart's blood, and if you don't keep to these terms, she'll avenge me."

"No one kills the Jabberwocky," Alice said, but her voice had lost its scornful confidence.

"If you don't bring Granny back, I'll come looking for her," Little Red warned. Never mind that she didn't know how to find Wonderland. Alice's eyes narrowed; she seemed to have the same thought. But Granny interjected.

"She'd follow us, all right. I found Wonderland, who says she couldn't? That would trouble things, wouldn't it? Your precious rule, upended by an unexpected intruder." Granny and Alice glared at each other, unflinching, as if reading memories in the others' eyes. "You wouldn't like that, Alice. Not at all." Granny spoke the name with contempt and for a moment, the woman seemed to shrink and quail, to become a scared young girl. Then she straightened.

"All right," she said, snapping the *t* like a whip. "If you're guilty, your grandbaby can fight the Jabberwocky. But don't try anything foolish, Red. My associate followed me here. He'll be watching this cottage and reporting back to me. Remember the Rabbit?"

Granny muttered something that sounded like "traitor" under her breath, but Little Red saw her lean body shudder with fright.

Little Red swallowed the ball of rage burning in her throat. It simmered in her stomach, fueling her plan. Alice underestimated people. She was an adult who believed she was in control.

If that's what she wants, I'll let her think she's right.

"Excuse me," she said in her most timid voice.

"What?" snapped Alice.

"Um, I met a wolf on my way here. I tricked him into chasing after a white rabbit I came across earlier. He seemed...a little bigger than average. The rabbit, I mean."

Alice nodded. "He's always late, but he's never slow. That wolf probably got the surprise of his life. You won't see him again, but he'll be around, watching you both." She strode to the door and opened it, looking around the cottage before giving its owner a final glare. Almost as an afterthought, she pulled something from her cloak and put it on the windowsill. It was a rose, veined and pale like an old, withered hand. "You're not the queen anymore, Red." With these final words, Alice left the cottage behind.

Granny sighed and embraced Little Red. "That's my brave girl! You're worth more than everything in Wonderland combined. But I only agreed to let you fight the Jabberwocky because I knew it would make Alice think twice. You mustn't fight it, Little Red, no matter what happens. Promise me that."

Little Red smiled. A queen had left her country and had a family, a granddaughter–herself! Granny was even more fascinating than she'd ever imagined. She fairly burst with pride. But the task at hand sobered her at once. "I can't promise you that, Granny. We'll think of a plan for getting you out of that trial. And just in case, tell me everything you know about this Jabberwocky. It's not immortal, is it?"

"No, but it's a magical creature, Little Red. It's much bigger than any wolf."

"Everything has a weakness, Granny. Wolves are easily led by their stomachs. Alice mistakes honesty for the whole story. She thinks she knows everything. The Jabberwocky has a chink in its armor somewhere, and if I need to, I'll find it."

The old woman frowned. "I don't like this at all, dearest. The throne was forced on me, and it'll twist anyone who strays too near it. I was glad to escape that country. It's a vast and strange place."

"So is this forest, and you taught me how to defend myself from its predators." Little Red took the scroll and the rose and tossed them into the fire. Then she opened her basket and gently pulled out the cakes. She grinned at the other thing she'd brought.

That wolf thought she was simply lucky. Alice thought she was a foolish, headstrong child. Little Red and her granny knew better. "Granny, let's make a soup. We're going to be talking for a long time."

She pulled the limp, fluffy body from the basket. She hadn't lied to that wolf; she'd just told it half the story, leveraging its weakness against it. Little Red had sent it chasing after a large white rabbit that would never report to Alice again.

Flower Heart

O nce, a young man with a secret went to make his fortune in
the city, as so many have before him. His name was Martin.

His eyes grew wide with wonder at the towering buildings and
winding streets. A multitude of smells assailed him, some pleasant,
most rank. As Martin and his mother had lived deep in the
country, he was surprised to see young men from all the
surrounding provinces. Fellow southerners with skin all shades of
copper like his own laughed with brown-skinned westerners,
tattooed easterners, and pale northerners. But this was no convivial
party, no celebration of good fortune; war had broken out with
the western kingdom and drawn many into its path, and the king
sought soldiers to fight his battles.

What else was there to do? *All my life my mother has coddled
me,* Martin thought, *and never let me tell anyone about my secret.
Here is my chance to prove I am as strong as everyone else.* He pulled
his coat tighter around the fluttering throb in his chest, a habitual
response to something he could not change, and found the tent
where men enlisted.

He had no idea there would be an examination until he was
told to wait for the doctor behind the tent and remove his shirt.
Martin obeyed the first command, trembling. His mother had once
told him about someone like him who had been denied work and

8

was eventually shunned by their whole village. He considered leaving for one panic-stricken moment, but the doctor appeared, bent and grumbling, and barely looked him over before declaring him fit for service. They gave him a uniform and Martin joined the ranks of new recruits.

He thought, naively, that the worst was over.

Training was brief and harsh. There were no grass or flowers in the muddy encampment, and anyway, no one spoke of such things unless they wanted derision or worse. Within a month, he was marching toward the battlefield, surrounded by hundreds of young men his age, most of them as eager to prove themselves as he was.

Army life was difficult and the march long. The other men often behaved coarsely and teased Martin for not joining in their crude joking. Sometimes, he feared his secret would become known, and then his mother might be right. *No one would accept me as I truly am,* he thought. He made a few friends, though he never told them of his secret. And then came the first battle.

When the fighting began, and the shouted orders, cannons, and gunfire made Martin's heart quail, he almost wished he had never enlisted. But it was too late to turn back. Amidst the explosions and the shouts and the blood, he fought valiantly. One by one, his friends fell at his side. Then something exploded in his ears, and a terrible pain tore through his hand. All went silent. All went dark.

Martin awoke after a long and dreamless sleep to find himself in a hospital cot. His missing left hand still throbbed with a dull, red pain. His whole body ached. The cries he heard from those around him were the cries of suffering and death. He fell in and out of slumber, now filled with dreams in which bullets blasted a hole through his chest and the wounds of the dead blossomed into crimson flowers. He burned with fever and chills. Sometimes he woke to see people carrying bodies away, and the cries around him grew fewer. He stopped wondering which belonged to men he knew.

Then one day, he stayed awake for several painful hours, and a weary, tight-lipped nurse handed him a paper.

"You've been expelled from the army," she said, "on account of your strange heart. It's a flower, or like enough, isn't it? We've no use for your kind here. Your aberration is weakness, a danger on the battlefield. What made you sign up in the first place?"

The nurse left without waiting for an answer. Martin shut his eyes and felt his strange heart fluttering in his chest, like a bird wearied with trying to escape. He could not hide his secret while walking between life and death.

At last, he recovered his strength and gathered his meager belongings. Ashamed and alone once again, Martin left the encampment to make what life he could in the city, where war's clawing hand had not yet wreaked destruction.

Perhaps it won't be so bad, he told himself. At least the soldiers that remained had believed him when he told them the loss of his hand was the reason for his expulsion. But they, like him, looked so hollow that perhaps it wouldn't have mattered if they had known the truth. Some of them would never be the same, even though their bodies were healed.

The nurse's paper he kept tucked into his coat as he walked. It was supposed to grant him employment, yet it had been marked with the words *Flower Heart*. He stopped himself from throwing it away once. Employment or not, he felt he had better keep it close, as if discarding the revealing paper would shout his secret to the world. *I am afraid,* he admitted to himself, *but am I more afraid of being discovered, or that the battlefield will never leave me?* He wondered this as he put miles between bloody destruction and himself, and he found no answers along the way.

Martin could not bring himself to visit his mother. Instead, he sent her a letter from a lonely village where he stopped for the night. A farmer let him sleep in his hayloft and thanked Martin for his money, but did not offer a second night. Autumn was turning to frost and the villagers were all lean and tired, fighting their own battles to survive.

At last, he reached the city, feeling neither relief nor fear this time. The chill only softened the smells of the streets. But nothing could soften the blow of war, not even distance. It seemed war had followed him to the city after all, just as the chill of winter had followed him from the battlefield. Martin passed the tent where he had enlisted and saw a sign on one of the posts which read, *Flower Hearts Need Not Apply.*

Are there many *more like me?* he thought in bewilderment. *Surely that sign did not appear on my behalf alone.* But a knot of men had gathered at the sign, pointing and laughing, so Martin went on his way.

People from all around the country lived in the city, for the variety of faces and features lay not just in the army. Many residents seemed tight-fisted or fearful, like the villagers; few people would hire a one-handed soldier. Some establishments demanded to see his army paper. Those that did swiftly turned him away once they saw the words *Flower Heart*.

He found intermittent work cleaning taverns and mucking stables, but it never lasted long. When he found the words *go home, flower heart, or we'll crush you,* scrawled in the muck of one stall, he left, his flower heart beating painfully in his chest.

He wrote to his mother here and there, when he had the money, always assuring her he was well. He never told her about his hand and hoped she would not see through his lies. The last letter he sent to her was full of aspirations that made him feel a fool, knowing he would not write to her again until he found employment.

This turned out to be impossible. He took to sleeping in doorways to save money, but the snow was falling faster, and his coat grew worn and his stump ached in the cold. Days later, a penny to his name and cold through, Martin found a tavern where he had not worked. He entered, in search of warmth, ale, and whatever kind of companionship he might find.

He hunched protectively over his drink as people around him made friendly arguments and bantered with one another. People came here to share jokes and laughter and gossip, eager to forget their own cares and the hardships of the world outside.

Have any of them fought in the war? Martin wondered. One man had a wooden leg. Another, an eyepatch. If there was any fellowship to be found, though, he sat outside of it.

Suddenly, a slurred voice rose above the noise. "Those damn flower hearts! Too weak for the king's war, so they stay here and take our jobs." A man, his red face shining with bitter anger, glared ahead. His two friends grinned into their ale, one adding, "and there's the truth!"

"There'll be nothing more for the men who come home proper heroes, more's the shame." He took another drink amidst muttered agreements.

Then where's my job? thought Martin, but he drank and was silent, and listened.

"Terrible business," said one of the grinning friends. "They can't stay in the army. It isn't natural, it isn't safe! But they're discharged before they can do any real good for the war either."

"Ah, but which is worse?" a new voice drawled, a voice of such languid arrogance that even the loud man, squinting and grumbling, stared at him and did not interrupt. The voice came from a pale, dark-haired young man who, but for his slowly blinking eyes, Martin would have guessed was sober. He raised a finger as if giving a lecture to an interested and paying audience and repeated his question. "Which is worse? A flower heart, or the greed that demands the lives of the country's young?"

"What would you know of it?" growled the red-faced man. "By the look of you, you've never worked a day in your life."

The pale young man chuckled. "Oh, I work. Only not at anything you'd recognize as such."

"Flower heart," the grinning man hissed. He was not grinning now.

"They aren't weak, you know," said the pale young man, his lazy position belied by the gleam in his eyes.

Perhaps he is sober after all. Martin tensed and watched.

"Aren't weak!" The loud man bellowed with laughter and stood, knocking over his chair. Whoever had been trying to ignore the scene wasn't ignoring them now; every eye in the tavern was trained on them. "Take me on, then! You're either one of them and asking for a beating, or you're no more than a lazy snot. Either way, you've got to prove yourself."

Martin nearly leaped to his feet. The pale young man rose like liquid smoke, lean as a winter's day. A moment later, a meaty hand connected with his face. Before Martin could blink, the pale young man lay sprawled on the floor, crimson ribboning from his long nose.

The red-faced man roared, swayed, and stumbled. His friends caught him. "You're a disgrace to the king and country," he spat. The tavern keeper, who had watched frowning behind the bar, hurried over like an anxious insect and ushered them out.

Everyone returned to their drinks immediately, their murmurs tinged with residual tension. No one paid the pale young man any attention. He sprang to his feet, paid his tab, and smiled once for no one. Then he walked out, sniffing and wiping his face, and he slammed the door shut.

Martin felt his flower heart wilt with disgust at himself. He had fought, he had seen men die, his friends had been blown to bits or had bled out next to him; why could he not help one poor idiot? He threw a coin on the table and hurried out.

Night was falling with the deepening cold, but he could see the drops of blood following a set of footsteps leading down an alley, and after these he hurried. After a few minutes, he could make out the figure of the pale young man ahead of him. *What am I going to do?* He asked himself, and had no answer. But after several turns down alleys that stank slightly less in winter than in summer, he admitted he was thoroughly lost. He met no one else. Sometimes he thought his quarry knew he was there, but the pale young man said nothing.

Then he stopped at a doorway and knocked. Martin sought cover behind a large, arthritic drainpipe. "Olivia," the pale young man said, "there's someone who wants in." He turned and grinned at Martin, who shrank against the wall and wondered if his flower heart would stop beating then and there.

"He does, does he?" said a smooth female voice at his elbow. Martin started. A young woman, brown-skinned and short, eyed him shrewdly beneath thick curling lashes. Her brown hair was braided in neat rows. "And what does he want with us, Alfred?"

"Please," Martin said, his voice shaking, "do you know any flower hearts?" *Why not?* he thought. *Who would hear me if I died here? I escaped death on the battlefield and in the medic tent; I suppose here would not be so surprising a place to die, and what have I got to lose?*

Alfred laughed and wiped his nose; his sleeve came away wet and dark. "Do you hold a grudge against them, too?"

"No. I've never met another, until now." He looked Alfred square in the face. Then with his right hand, he drew his shirt collar aside to reveal the strangely pulsating skin.

Alfred glanced at Olivia, who nodded. "You'd better come in, then," he said, and he sounded dead sober.

They led him through the door and into a large, dark room, an abandoned storehouse of sorts, furnished with rough tables and last century's sofas. Bright paintings hung on one wall and curtains partitioned parts of the room. Lamplight softened the hard edges. In a corner, two people rose from one of the tables.

"It's all right. He's one of us," Olivia assured them. Then she turned to Martin. "Welcome to our illustrious Society of Flower Hearts," she said.

She introduced him to the other two. There was George, an easterner who had been run out of his village before the war; now he did odd jobs for grocers and wrote the stories he had kept safe since childhood. There was Aletha, tall, square, and red-haired, who would not speak of what had happened to her. She did not speak at all. But there was a violin in the corner that she took up and played, and she sang with a voice that made Martin feel warm and safe, and he saw that the others felt the same.

Olivia used to run messages for an official but left when the war broke out, before she was discovered, and now organized hospital supplies for the front. And she painted. The paintings were hers, more colorful and storied than anything Martin had ever seen. Several city officials who lived as though the war would change nothing for them had bought a few and paid well, thinking they had purchased the work of a far-away artist working in some gilded hall. Alfred had been turned out of the army, like Martin, and like him, had lost his last job. When Martin asked where his artistry lay, he only grinned.

Then they asked Martin for his story. He told it, and for the first time, he wept for those who had died, for the bitterness of the war which had taken so much. He wept for his mother, for keeping so much from her. When he was done, Aletha gave him a handkerchief and a silent look of compassion that spoke louder than words.

"We are all artists, in some form or fashion," said Olivia. She nodded at Aletha and her violin. "Some people want what we create. But this war doesn't want us or our flower hearts. It will need us, though, when all those men return home. Sooner or later, people will understand that what they fear and discard is the very thing they need." Her smile broadened into a grin. "But we create a world for ourselves first."

"You'll have to work, like the rest of us," Alfred said to Martin. "We have contacts throughout the city. Sometimes work is hard to find and we go hungry. But I suspect you'll manage."

"I have no very great skills," Martin said. "And I should write to my mother. She must be sick with worry."

Olivia raised an eyebrow. "No skills that you know of yet," she said, smiling again. "I believe we have paper somewhere. You may stay if you wish, Martin."

Martin felt his heart soften and stir, like the flowers he had seen open once after a spring rain. Alfred put an arm around his shoulder. "Of course, he'll stay," he said.

And of course, Martin did.

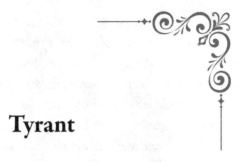

Tyrant

Walking home through the woods, her quiver full of slender branches, Mabyn had almost reached the cottage when the soldiers found it first. The sudden clank of metal armor doused her with cold fear. She slunk behind a tree and watched, the back of the cottage obscuring her view.

At least two dozen men congregated before her home. Where was Gryffudd? She told herself he was safe, that he would be gone on an errand, but it was a futile denial. She knew he was home. She knew why the soldiers had come.

She flinched as wood and metal squealed, signaling someone had thrown open the front door. There were sounds of a brief scuffle. Mabyn bit back a cry as Gryffudd appeared, led by two soldiers. She had only four metal-tipped arrows among the unformed branches at her back. It wasn't enough.

The captain stepped forward, a large man whose armor bore the queen's snow flower emblem. He was a mindless follower, as loyal to money and esteem as he was to his liege, yet eager and swift to follow Vanora's commands. He regarded Gryffudd with disdain.

"The queen has heard rumors," he said. "She's no longer satisfied with the tales of the princess' kidnap and death. And here you are, proof that they are false tales indeed. If you're alive, then so must be the princess you tried to steal." He stepped closer, lowering his voice so that Mabyn had to strain to hear it. "No traitor captain can stop the queen's plans. Even now, a marriage to the northern prince would strengthen the kingdom, and the queen will have her way. Tell me who hired you and where she is."

Gryffudd said nothing, his back straight and proud. The captain planted a fist in his stomach. Mabyn clutched at the tree and gritted her teeth as he wheezed and coughed. They dragged him away, slinging him unceremoniously over a horse, and the company rode from the tiny clearing toward the direction of the castle. The horses, men, and shields bearing the white flower vanished.

How she hated that flower. That something so innocuous as a delicate blossom had become the symbol of tyranny made her blood fizz and sting. While it was said that spirits haunted the queen's tower, the unsettled remains of her sorcery, it was the snow flower and all it stood for that repulsed Mabyn the most.

She scarcely waited for the pounding of hoofs to fade before rushing into the cottage and seizing what she needed. She discarded the small knife in her vest and strapped the larger one in its leather sheath to her waist. Provisions, water skin, bandages, healing salve. They would torture her love for information, and he would die before he gave her away.

I will reach him first.

She followed the horses' hoof prints easily along the muddy, narrow track. It was a day's journey to the castle on horseback. On foot, she would arrive at midnight, back at the place she'd hoped never to set foot in again.

When Queen Vanora had betrothed her to the northern prince a year ago, only Gryffudd had had confidence they could get out of it. *Go with the company,* he'd said. *I'll come for you. Trust me, Mabyn.*

I do trust you, she'd replied. He was the only sure thing in her life besides the weight of ruling. She never doubted his cunning or his love, but, trapped between Vanora and the northern prince, Mabyn feared whatever plan Gryffudd concocted would have little chance of succeeding. Still, she might as well grasp her last thread of hope while she could. What did she have to lose by trusting an impossible scheme?

So she'd said goodbye to her home of wealth and stone, riding with the soldiers into the north woods. She had felt Vanora's eyes on her back as she watched from her tower—the unseen, all-seeing witch queen of Elis.

By nightfall, she reached the place of the attack. She recalled Gryffudd breaking through the tree line, disguised as a huntsman. His shouting and volley of arrows threw the small company into disarray, giving his band of disguised guards time to do their work. Mabyn's shock had been real at first. Under the cover of his friends' attack, Gryffudd had pulled Mabyn off her horse, hoisted her over his shoulder, and melted into the forest. But two of the company's arrows had hit their marks.

While the other huntsmen had fled, the queen's soldiers took one look at the fallen princess and her kidnapper and left them for dead. They hadn't counted on the huntsmen coming back and tending the wounded couple until they healed. They hadn't known that no one had hired Gryffudd. They hadn't known he and Mabyn had been in love for years.

The hunstmen, their lives as queen's guards forfeit for their loyalty to a traitor, had dispersed throughout the kingdom and beyond, into the farthest reaches of Cambria. Mabyn and Gryffudd would soon follow suit. *This time tomorrow, we'll be far away,* thought Mabyn, *and my stepmother will never hunt us again. She will no longer force us to live in fear.*

Mabyn hurried past the spot and let the memories follow her. She plunged off the road and into the underbrush to avoid being detected, confident in the tracking skills she'd learned over the past few months. They had been simple times, full of hard work she was unaccustomed to. But spent with Gryffudd, it was all she could ask for.

Now, she was going back to the place she had left. This time, their roles were reversed. He had taken her from a life she despised and offered paradise. It was her turn to rescue him.

She didn't rest once along the way. She tried not to let herself think about what they were doing to Gryffudd or imagine his pained cries. How had the soldiers found them after all these months? Had the queen forced their whereabouts from the friar who had married them in secret? Had she captured one of the rogue guards? The thoughts drove her onward as if she could hear the cries of their tortured confessions in her head.

She smelled the castle before she saw it. The reeking water in the moat, the odor of horses, dirty straw, and filth—the stench of the invisible lives of those who ran the castle while Queen Vanora plotted and hid. Mabyn may have forgotten how bad the smell was, or maybe it was far worse than it used to be.

Entrance by the main gate was impossible, but not problematic. The fugitive princess slid around behind the castle keep, pushing through waist-high plants and weeds, until she found a fallen log that balanced across the moat and led to a hole in the back courtyard wall. Mabyn grinned despite the circumstances as she walked nimbly across it, squeezed through the tiny opening, and descended through the stone bowels. She had used this way to meet with Gryffudd many times. Now they would escape this way, too.

The smell intensified once she entered the courtyard, but the sight filled her with horror. This place was a small village, housing servants and the shops that provided necessary services to maintain the castle. As a girl, Mabyn had spent as much time here as she had her dark and ancient home. But everything had changed.

No torches burned this late, and Mabyn's eyes were accustomed to the darkness. She could make out stone walls crumbling into disrepair. Shop fronts, once clean and brightly painted, were now dingy and muddy. Either the elements or people had broken up the courtyard cobblestones, leaving muddy pits that no cart could manage. Mabyn walked along as if in a trance, stopping to stare at the smithy. Someone was awake after all. Smoke rose from the chimney, the smell blotted out by the reek of animals and refuse.

Mabyn resisted the impulse to go inside and see if old Tomas still worked the bellows. She couldn't risk bringing harm to the blacksmith who had laughed at her dirt-smudged nose and let her try the bellows for herself, tying his heavy apron around her in an effort to protect her dress. For all she knew, every servant she had ever spoken to had forgotten her. It should remain that way. Even if she had arrived in broad daylight, no one would recognize her in her current garb, and she needed to rely on all her hard-won stealth. It was the guards she would have to outwit and evade now.

She found the old cracks in the wall and clambered right up to the small western tower, her hands and feet remembering every hold and dent in the stone. Mabyn swung herself in through the tall, narrow window. The moment she stood up, a clattering noise made her spin around.

"My lady!"

The old man stared at her through filmy eyes, his frail body trembling. "Are you a ghost?"

"No, Niclas. It's me. I'm truly here." Mabyn stooped and picked up the pieces of broken crockery, giving herself a moment to recover and think. Why was the queen forcing her elderly servant to work such late hours? She hadn't wanted to encounter anyone, not even this gentle soul.

"Does the queen know you're alive?" Niclas asked, his voice warbling with age and innocence.

She handed him the crockery, then reached out and gently squeezed his shoulder. He felt so painfully thin. "No. And she never will. What are you doing here so late, Niclas? You should be sleeping."

"Queen Vanora sent me to bring her some water, my lady."

A strange memory niggled at the back of her mind. Her stepmother had been cold, distant, and relentless in all things she set her mind to. But Mabyn couldn't recall Vanora ever using a cruel word with her servants. She never had to, as most feared her and obeyed her without question. Had the queen's behavior worsened since she'd gone?

"At this hour?" Mabyn frowned. "Surely she has a maid for that."

"The queen is a tortured soul, Princess Mabyn. She is trapped, in a way. Few are willing to go near her now." Now he patted her arm affectionately, as if his words explained everything.

Indignation rose in Mabyn, tightening her throat. The queen had magic and power and wealth; whatever losses she'd suffered, she'd never suffered to hear her stepdaughter's pleas. Niclas had always been too soft-hearted. It had blinded him to how things truly were.

"She chose to marry my father. She chose this place," she said. *If only she had chosen to listen to me, just once.* She pushed the thought away. Time was running out. "Niclas, I must find the dungeons. She's taken someone I love. I need to rescue him."

In the torchlight, uncertainty wavered across Niclas' face. "Queen Vanora keeps the only set of keys," he said.

"I'll break in."

He shook his head. "Princess, you can't. She's put spells on all the chambers. You'll need the keys and the queen's help."

Mabyn flexed her hands into fists. She had hoped to never see her stepmother again. But if magic stood between her and Gryffudd, she had no other choice.

"Where is the queen?"

Niclas sighed. "In her chambers, princess."

"Thank you, Niclas. Go get some sleep." She patted his arm again and smiled sadly.

"Will you bring her the water, then?"

"I'll find a maid to do it, yes."

Rheumy eyes regarded her with a clarity that forced Mabyn's own gaze to falter. "If you were here again, my lady, we'd see the castle restored," the old man said. "Things would be like they were when your father lived."

Mabyn shook her head. Life was more complicated than that. It was too late to change anything. "I can't live that life anymore, Niclas. I'm sorry." She gave him a half-hearted smile and turned away before she could see the disappointment on his face.

She met no guards along the way and only one servant, easily evaded by stepping into a darker corridor. The queen must rely on the terror of her magic rather than brute force to keep herself safe. Vanora's chambers were tucked away in a part of the castle Mabyn was less familiar with, and she took a few wrong turns. She had no intention of bringing the queen anything, though the resolve gave her guilt when she thought of Niclas. She pushed the unpleasantness away and rounded another corner.

There, at last: the final staircase at the end of the hall, identified as the entrance to Vanora's chambers by that awful snow flower emblem carved in the door at the top. Mabyn began her ascent when a memory washed over her like the cold night air.

She felt the tight panic in her chest from the only night she'd followed the queen here. They had just finished an intense and distressing council meeting. The north was pressuring for a marriage and her stepmother had agreed to the offered terms with the tight-lipped, white-faced expression Mabyn had come to associate with cold resolution. Her stepmother had given her away as if she were a piece of jewelry to a man twice her age and known for his violence.

Mabyn had followed her up this very staircase, shouting for her to listen, begging her to change her mind. But Queen Vanora hadn't listened. She never wanted to listen. She had flown up these stairs as if her life depended on it, through the first door, and

Mabyn remembered catching a glimpse of the queen's reflection in a tall mirror just before a second door slammed shut. The pale, drawn features had hardened into something inhuman and cruel, transforming Vanora's face till it was barely recognizable.

Mabyn shivered at the memory. It served as a reminder to move quickly before the queen had a chance to react. This was her only defense against sorcery.

She crept up the stairs and swiftly palmed the knife from its sheath. Breathing a prayer that the door remained well-oiled, she pushed against the wooden frame.

It swung inward without so much as a creak. The room was empty of people and furnishings, as she knew it would be. The queen kept everyone out.

Silence filled the room, but a light shone under the second door, a shadow wavering back and forth across it. Mabyn examined the hinges. These, too, had been oiled. She thought of Gryffudd, drew a deep breath for courage, and slowly pushed the door forward.

A tall, black-robed figure stood with her back to the door, so still she could have been carved of stone. Torchlight glittered on her silver crown, each tiny point sharp as a spear tip. Mabyn could see her reflection in the mirror.

The queen's cold eyes were blank, drained of expression. She might have been dead but for the slow rise and fall of her chest. Then, like the creep of mist rising from the ground, the queen's reflection wavered, shifting into the cruel image Mabyn remembered.

"Let me go." The queen's voice was a whisper from still lips, though the reflection remained still at first. Then its features twisted into a horrible grin.

"Your service is not yet through." It spoke with Vanora's features, but this was not her voice. A shiver danced down Mabyn's spine. "You, and all you achieve, belong to me."

"This is not what I wanted." Vanora's voice was quiet.

"This is what you chose."

A cry escaped Vanora's lips. She seemed to strain against some invisible force. A vein stood out on her smooth temple and sweat beaded on her upper lip. The face in the mirror laughed as her efforts died.

"Do you think it is so simple? The price you paid for power is not one you can regain."

Mabyn broke from her shock. Yes, she really had heard those words. There was indeed a spirit in the tower. But this was no mere phantom, fated to obey the queen's every whim.

The source of her power is in the mirror itself.

In a flash, Mabyn made her choice. She squeezed the knife once, gauged the distance, and hurled it with precision.

The queen's eyes widened. The blade met its mark in a melody of shattering glass. The tall figure collapsed onto a floor of broken shards.

Mabyn bolted forward and lifted her motionless stepmother from the ground. Vanora's eyes fluttered open, searching her stepdaughter's face. "Mabyn?"

The usually stern voice sounded oddly confused and young. For a moment, the princess saw another facet of her stepmother, one she had never seen before: frightened, innocent, naive. It was almost like looking at a younger version of herself.

She helped her to her feet and stepped back, turning her attention to the destroyed mirror. It gaped like an eye of the dead. Something subtle yet palpable shifted in the room. Mabyn drew a deep, painful breath as if a crushing weight had lifted from her chest.

"Why?" she demanded. It was the only word she could form.

Vanora blinked at the mirror, her pale face now lined and tired. She wiped a thin hand across her brow.

"I don't know where it came from," she said quietly. "It arrived after your father's death. I was so scared, so alone. The mirror...helped me to make decisions. It made me feel powerful. A submissive spirit dwelt in it, I believed. Something I could bend to suit my needs. By the time something felt wrong...it was too late. It drew me in until it controlled me." She sighed, then straightened, regaining some of her regal composure, but anger flared hot in Mabyn's gut. She hadn't come to hear a tale of woe. Better to keep this encounter short and to the point.

"You had Gryffudd arrested. Give me the keys. I want him free. Now." She stepped forward and retrieved her knife in one sweeping motion, never taking her eyes off the other woman's face, boring into her eyes with her own fierce gaze. "I set you free. A life for a life, Vanora."

But Vanora wasn't looking at her, seemed not to be listening again. "How many lives have I ruined?" she whispered. "What have I done?"

Lives? Were the kingdom's power and image not her primary concerns? Did this cold and distant woman truly care about anyone other than herself? Mabyn stepped forward.

"All I wanted was to marry the man I love," she said. She had never seen her stepmother so vulnerable, nor act with any regret. It was so foreign that it seemed genuine. But a sorceress might be as good at playing the penitent ruler as she was at practicing magic. She had power before the mirror; maybe now she only wanted to protect herself. Mabyn kept her grim visage in place. "He shouldn't be in the dungeons. You can't make me stay or marry any prince now. Give me the keys."

Vanora returned to the present and fumbled with something in her robe. "Here," she said, holding out the brass ring with its many keys.

"Now remove the spells."

"There aren't any. Rumors, I suppose. I've spun my share of them over the years. It helped protect my image."

Mabyn took the keys and turned to go. This could all be a trap, but she would rather take her chances in the dungeon than remain with Vanora. She wasn't comfortable with her own confusion surrounding her stepmother's unusual display of frailty.

"Mabyn, wait."

She paused, half turned, and the queen went on.

"Do you know, my own stepmother was rumored to have a mirror. I'd forgotten that. I never thought I would become like her." Vanora shook her head, her brows furrowed. "Where do these mirrors come from, Mabyn? How do they know we are vulnerable?" Her question was not rhetorical; she spoke in a calm voice, but there was a desperate undercurrent beneath.

Could any monarch really be so naive?

"We are women," Mabyn said. "In our world, that alone marks us as vulnerable. A position of authority marked you as dangerous. I never wanted that burden." She didn't try to hide the bitterness in her voice.

"But you *are* a princess. Just as I am a queen."

"When did that ever unite us? I was always too much for you. You never wanted my opinion. I wanted out, Vanora."

Mabyn waited for a reprimand, a denial. But Vanora paused as if considering her stepdaughter's words. Her long, thin fingers worried the hem of her robe. When she spoke, it was almost a plea.

"I want your opinion now. I know I ask too much, Mabyn. I know we...don't often see eye to eye. But you know this kingdom in ways I can't comprehend. And there will always be people who send mirrors until someone else stops them. There will always be naive maidens to whom no one explains the world, because they're too busy grooming them to marry the right person." She inhaled, exhaled sharply. "I'm afraid I want more than your opinion. I'm asking you to come back and help me rule."

This might be the nearest thing to an apology I've ever received. Mabyn almost laughed at the thought. *Of course she* would *couch it in a way that pulls me back to the role I left behind.*

Still...she'd heard news during the last few months in the woods, whispers of magic and treachery festering beyond the kingdom of her youth. All suspicions pointed to a person for whom she had no love.

"The northern prince," she said. "I heard rumors he was a magician. Not as powerful as a sorcerer, but you might start there, if you're going to look for the source of dangerous looking glasses." She gripped the keys and turned to leave, but something made her pause.

Old Niclas. The courtyard. Tomas.

A pang of something pierced her heart. It was so foreign that she couldn't recognize it; it also drew her back to Gryffudd, and she and Gryffudd didn't belong here, not anymore.

Yet one question wouldn't let her leave without asking it aloud.

"Why did you send the guards to find me?" Mabyn demanded.

Again, the queen looked at the mirror.

"I'm not sure how much of that was me and how much of that was..." She gestured at the yawning, gold frame, and again lost herself in thought before continuing with a wry smile. "It's true that I never liked being a stepmother. I didn't have the best experience with my own. But I am glad you're alive. With all my mistakes, I needed to know that something good had survived."

Mabyn grunted to cover her surprise. "Mistakes are hardly what I'd call them."

Vanora nodded gravely. Again, she made no denial. Her silence was not one of coldness, but of sobriety, perhaps even grief.

Wonders may never cease.

Another strange thought dawned on Mabyn. This foreign pang she felt was homesickness. For the castle, the place she'd known and even loved a little, while her father lived. The people who'd been kind to her. Even with the mirror shattered, they weren't out of danger yet.

Maybe she could come home. Maybe Gryffudd would agree to stay at her side, despite everything. She wouldn't do it without him.

It was a lot to think about. No matter her final choice, this was no simple decision, and she would make it on her own time, on her own terms.

"A month," she said, watching surprise cross Vanora's face. "I will give you my answer in a month."

"Very well." The queen nodded. "Do you know where to find the dungeons?"

It was Mabyn's turn to nod. "I'm not the one who spent all her time in a tower," she said.

She clutched the keys in her hand, focusing on the sharp metal biting into her flesh, and only looked at them when she was halfway down the castle's dampest stairwell. A sharp edge had pierced her finger. The petals of a snow flower formed the pointed tip of the key's bow, just as they formed the spikes on Vanora's crown. A drop of her own blood had stained them red.

Strange, holding a symbol of tyranny that will open the door to escape. Escape and, even stranger, the possibility of return.

The dungeons smelled worse than the courtyards, but it was easy to find Gryffudd's cell. It was the only one that didn't emit the sounds of mice scampering across the floor. He scuffled to his feet in the straw as Mabyn twisted the key in the lock and drew the heavy door open without bothering to retrieve it. She flung herself into his arms, a sob wrenching from her throat; he was solid, warm, whole.

Home.

"My hero," he whispered into her hair. They kissed hungrily, as if they'd been apart weeks instead of hours.

Gryffudd drew back reluctantly, his eyes darting to the doorway before searching her face in the darkness. "What about the queen?"

"Don't worry about her. You're not hurt?" Her fingers traced his face, felt his arms, his clothes; she could find no blood, no new signs of struggle on him.

"No. They dumped me here and haven't been back since." He took her face in his hands, brows furrowed. "What's going on, Mabyn? Why did she hunt for us in the first place? Something about this is very strange."

Vanora hadn't lied about the spells, and no one had hurt Gryffudd. Still, this would be difficult for him, for both of them. Mabyn drew a deep breath. "I went to find my stepmother to get the keys. There was a spell on her. I broke it. And...we spoke." She watched his face for signs of incredulity and saw only alert focus. "Things aren't quite all they seemed, Gryffudd. Something bigger than Vanora is at work here. Someone is endangering the kingdom."

"What do you mean?"

"The spell on her didn't come from our kingdom, and I have an idea who is behind it. She wants me to come back and help her stop them. She wants me to resume my role."

He made an incredulous sound, his eyes searching hers. "How do you know she hasn't drawn up this whole scheme herself?"

Mabyn took his hands from her face and held them. Who could blame his questions, his doubts? She would've had them too if not for the scene at the mirror. "Vanora could have killed or imprisoned me. She didn't order any harm to you. She wanted to make sure I was alive after hearing rumors that I hadn't died in the attack. The captain has always followed his ego as much as her orders. She's never evoked warm feelings in me. We don't have to like her, Gryffudd. But this is bigger than us, and..."

"And being back is pulling at you."

She nodded. "I worry that I walked away from too much."

Silence filled the cell, heavy with uncertainty and questions too large yet to name. Mabyn felt as if it would smother her.

Gryffudd looked down at their joined hands. "I think I've always known you would face this decision," he said quietly. "I knew we hadn't truly put this behind us."

"How?" Now it was Mabyn's time to be surprised.

He shrugged. "No one can outrun their past. The more you ignore it, the larger it becomes. Sooner or later, everyone's got to face up to it."

Mabyn stood silent, gripping his hands as if for dear life. "You knew, all this time, and you still risked everything for me?"

He nodded.

"Why?"

"Because I love you, Mabyn. It's that simple."

Love had always been simple with Gryffudd, straightforward and clear, even when nothing else was. And yet love was not love if it bound anyone against their will.

"You freed me, knowing neither of us could be truly free," Mabyn said. She inhaled shakily, past the burgeoning pain in her heart. "This may be my past, but you are my future. I don't want any life without you in it. Still, if you don't–"

"Stop." Gryffudd's voice was a whisper. "I don't want to hear it. Just answer me this: how long?"

She blinked at him, unable to speak.

"I mean," he said slowly, a hesitant smile on his face, "how long did you make her wait for your decision?"

"I said I would tell her in a month. That's a month to watch her and gather information." Mabyn squeezed his hands again, hesitant relief expanding in her chest. "I'll take my time deciding and I won't do it without you, Gryffudd. After all we've fought for, almost losing each other, almost dying. Wherever I go, I want it to be with you. Trust me on that."

His smile seemed to light the dark. Was it possible that home could be both a person and a place? Maybe one was her anchor in the other, wherever that place might be, whatever burdens came with it. She felt that in that moment, she had never loved him more.

"I do trust you, Mabyn. Now I'm ready to go."

She flung her arms around him again, parting only to steal another kiss. Then, hand in hand, they left the cell behind.

The Dragon of Shining Valley

Dresden was the fiercest creature the people of Shining Valley had seen for a hundred years. They did not know the creature's name was Dresden. They only knew a dragon had arrived on the mountains one day, striking terror in the hearts of everyone who could see the smoke curling from the tallest peak.

They saw flashes of red scales and wings when the dragon stirred, the sure signs of a fire breather. The villagers uttered prayers to every deity they could remember. Then they sent young maidens as a peace offering, just to be sure. One can never be too careful with dragons.

But Dresden didn't eat the young maidens, nor did they receive so much as a burn mark. Dresden preferred the occasional well-roasted pig or sheep. What she really loved to eat were the fire berries that grew on the mountains. These, she had been taught, gave her the hottest dragon-breath flames, and so she ate them almost every day.

Yes, she; not only did Dresden despise the thought of eating human flesh, but she was a female, named by one very disappointed father who had hoped for male offspring to carry on the family legacy. This was perhaps the main reason for her leaving home and settling above the valley. And it proved to be a good one, for a dragon. But neither fire berries nor livestock could fix Dresden's most pressing problem, which was loneliness.

The maidens she sent back home to their families, who, unable to grasp the concept of a dragon who would not eat tender young maiden, made up elaborate stories of how their girls had outwitted the monster. And still the villagers prayed.

To Dresden's delight, a few of these girls returned. They came out of curiosity. They didn't seem to fear her harsh dragon's voice or fire-breath, and life in a tiny village can be very dull when your inevitable path in life leads to marriage to a second or third cousin. When Dresden engaged these girls in conversation, a few returned for friendship.

Marigold, a girl with golden brown skin and smooth black hair, visited the most often. She introduced Dresden to the joys of reading. Delighted to find someone who appreciated the forgotten poets of old, the girl spent many afternoons basking in the summer sun with the dragon, reading words strung together like jewels on a queen's necklace.

Dresden listened to the music of Marigold's reading in delight. And for a time, she was happy. She didn't mind that her cave was dark and damp when she had company. Listening to poetry made her forget that she was a disappointing dragon. She could almost imagine herself a girl, like her friends.

Once, as she was listening to Marigold with her eyes closed, the girl's voice trailed off. Dresden opened her eyes and found her friend's gaze fixed somewhere far away. The view from her cave was mostly of the valley below. But sometimes, on especially clear days, one could see a trail carving its way between two peaks, leading out into the wide world beyond the village. It was in this direction that Marigold's eyes were fixed.

"What is it, Marigold?" Dresden asked.

The girl sighed. "Do you ever wonder what life could be like somewhere else?"

"Not really." Dresden shifted her scaly arms and repositioned her head on them. "I flew over other villages on my way here. They all look the same from the sky."

"Lucky dragon. You can fly wherever you wish." Marigold smiled affectionately, but Dresden was alarmed to see a trace of sadness in her eyes.

"And where would you go, if you could?" she asked.

The girl gazed along the road, then down at the half-forgotten book in her lap. "Somewhere, there are universities brimming with books and people who appreciate them," she said. "If I weren't a simple village girl, I might be able to go to one."

Dresden felt a little of Marigold's own sadness settle in her dragon's heart at the thought. "You're not simple at all," she said. "And if you weren't a village girl, I never would have met you."

"True on both counts." The girl's smile held less sadness in it this time. "And what about you? Wouldn't you like to see the world on those magnificent wings of yours?"

Dresden thought for a moment. "No," she answered. "I've seen all I want to. I'm content to fly over this valley. My home is here, and you are here, dear Marigold. Oh, promise me you'll not leave? I would be so sad without you."

Marigold reached out a hand and stroked Dresden's scaly head between her horns. "There's little chance of that," she said. "Still, I suppose we can't help wanting what we can't have now and then."

This proved true in ways neither girl nor dragon could have imagined.

Not everyone in the village of Shining Valley felt this way, however. As weeks passed, fewer and fewer girls came by Dresden's cave. Some were simply too busy to make the journey. Some decided that the climb was too much. Whatever their reasons, most of them stopped coming altogether. Yet Dresden and Marigold maintained their reading sessions. Marigold risked a scolding or extra chores for being away so long, and was told no one would marry a girl who spent all her time wandering around, but this did not bother her at all.

Then one day, as Dresden basked in the sun and Marigold read love sonnets aloud, the dragon looked up and saw the answer to the villagers' prayers. He swooped down over a far mountain dressed in clothes of changing light, and from all around him fell cascades of rain as if he rode a tide of falling water. He appeared human in form, though his skin was blue and gray. Dresden knew what he was. That didn't stop her from falling in love immediately.

"How does one win the heart of a god?" she asked Marigold.

Marigold, being human, couldn't see the gods. But she was well versed in poetry and understood what had happened. The villagers, fearing fire and smoke, had prayed especially to the god of rain, and he had answered.

"I'm not entirely sure," Marigold began. A damp breeze ruffled her hair and sweetened the air around them. "But it might involve a gift."

"What gift could a rain god want?" Dresden asked, spellbound.

The girl wrinkled her nose, though Dresden didn't see it, and it might only have been in thought. "Plants? Rain waters the earth, after all, or what else is there for a rain god to do? I might have a poem about it somewhere."

Dresden didn't really hear Marigold's answer. By the time the rain god had left, evening was fast turning to night. The girl had gone home, too. The dragon felt so strangely bereft that she didn't swoop down on her leathery wings in search of dinner.

The next morning, she gathered her strength and went to the high forest in the mountains where the best fire berries grew. They were the best gift she could imagine. She brought a mound of them back and waited outside her cave. But the rain god never appeared.

When Marigold came back that afternoon, she found a dejected Dresden lying next to a clump of withered berries.

"No luck yet?" she asked her scaled friend sympathetically. Dresden shook her long, toothy head. "Well then," said Marigold, holding up a burlap sack, "I hate to see you looking forlorn. Here is something that may help. Good fortune for us! I found more poetry."

The girl and the dragon pored over the books all afternoon, trying to find something that would catch a rain god's attention. At last, in the moldering pages of a slim book belonging to a poet who had once lived in the valley, Marigold found the tale of a woman who drew the attention of the rain god by standing in a mountain stream. Dresden was elated.

"I know just where one such stream is, high on a peak," she said.

Marigold climbed on her back and the two of them flew to the place. It was a small cliff jutting from the mountain, just large enough for a few scattered trees and a determined mountain stream to make its way down. The girl hid herself behind a tree while the dragon settled in the midst of the clear, icy water, shivering and watching the sky expectantly. She did not have long to wait.

The rain god glided across the valley in a shimmer of blues and grays. Dresden longed to call to him, but she was so cold from the water that all that came out of her throat was a wisp of smoke. She watched him sweep around the valley, letting curtains of rain fall, until at last, he flew off between distant peaks. Dresden felt even sadder than before.

"It must be my fire," she said to Marigold. "How could a rain god have anything to do with a smoky, flame-breathing creature like me?"

"Perhaps it isn't meant to be," said Marigold. Dresden didn't notice the girl's thoughtful, worried gaze. "Come, let's go back to your cave. I must go home, and you're chilled through."

That night, Dresden ate a wandering sheep instead of fire berries. The next morning, before it was light, she went back to the stream; she waited in it until her clawed toes grew numb and she shivered so loudly her red scales rang like cymbals. But oh, how her heart soared when at last the flying god approached once more, bringing his curtains of rain. This time, when she called him, her voice came out in a thin, wavering note, like a singer testing a new song. And to Dresden's shock, the rain god turned once around the valley and sailed toward her until he alighted just beside the stream.

He was just as glorious at this proximity. No, even more so, thought Dresden, who swallowed and held her breath. Today, his tunic-like clothes were the same grayish blue as his skin. He looked like an impossibly beautiful man. None of this bothered Dresden in the least. When he spoke, his voice was melodious and low.

"Beautiful dragon," he said, "why did you call me?"

Suddenly shy, Dresden lowered her long nose and glanced at him through curly eyelashes. "I wanted to meet you," she said. "I hope I didn't alarm you."

"Not at all. I am only surprised you can see me. Few mortals ever do." He smiled. "You must be very rare indeed. What is your name?"

"Dresden," said the she-dragon. "What is yours?"

He spoke in a fluting language Dresden could not understand. It sounded like a distant storm. "Oh dear, I don't think I can say that," she said. "What might I call you?"

"Why not simply call me Rain?" he answered, and smiled. Dresden beamed back at him.

They spoke at length then, asking one another about all they had seen. They spoke of flight and the sky and how different the air felt to them.

"I am a very unimportant rain god," Rain told her, "for I have never left this place, save to go home. The valley is my sole domain." He asked Dresden of the places she'd seen on her journey to Shining Valley. The she-dragon, thinking him anything but unimportant, told him all she could, and he listened with rapt attention.

The sun reached its zenith unnoticed and sank, and the evening chill gathered around them. When at last he departed, Dresden soared home. What joy she felt! Despite the lack of feeling in her cold limbs, she was thrilled. At last, she had met the rain god, and he was as wonderful as she could have imagined.

The next morning, she returned to the same place. The rain god also returned, and they spoke together for much of the day. This time, he noticed she was cold.

"Why not step out of the water, gentle dragon?" he said. "I hate to see you uncomfortable."

Dresden did so, and Rain sat at a distance, for steam rose painfully from his skin if he sat too close. Over time, this distance bothered her, so she took to sitting in the stream as often as she could stand it, and Rain would come and stand near her so that she could see his stormy eyes grow bright or dark depending on the conversation. And all below them, curtains of ceaseless rain fell over the valley.

This went on all summer. The god's moods matched the weather, or perhaps they influenced it. Sometimes, he talked on and on while the rain fell in steady sheets. Other times, he flung his musings from topic to topic, like small, sudden rain-bursts that vanished as soon as they started. And sometimes, he sat quietly and listened to Dresden, gathering his thoughts like the slow burgeoning of rain clouds, waiting to set them free when she was tired of talking.

Rain knew nothing of poetry, so Dresden happily introduced him to some of her favorite verses. But he found the thoughts of humans absurd and small, so she ceased to bring it up, telling herself it didn't matter much. They began to run up against the edges of all the things they had discussed; Dresden had described many times all the places she'd seen, and Rain had demonstrated all the kinds of squalls he could stir up. Though Rain tried to teach her his strange, fluting language, she could never quite seem to get the feel of it.

Still, she was happy just to meet with him. And if Dresden returned to her cave at night cold and hardly saw Marigold, she considered those things not at all. Not at all, that is, until one day, when the girl returned.

The she-dragon had just landed outside her cave in a flutter of delight when she spied Marigold sitting at her usual spot. She held no books and she looked rather soggy. Locks of limp hair dripped down her back and her dress hung damply on her frame.

"Marigold! How lovely to see you," said Dresden.

"I'm happy you think so," said the girl, "but I fear you won't like my news."

Dresden tried to light a fire for both of them, but hours of sitting in a stream had weakened her flame. She coughed on the attempt. A tiny spark burst from her mouth, sizzled, and vanished.

"The villagers were happy with the unseasonal rain at first," Marigold said, "but it's gone on so long that nothing can dry out. Our food is going bad and we sleep in damp clothes. The mud is inescapable."

"Oh," said Dresden. She was feeling uncomfortable—and it had nothing to do with the chill. She was happy to see Marigold, and felt suddenly guilty for not seeing her sooner, and she felt something else she could not name.

"Some people are ill from the damp. If the rain god doesn't leave us alone, our whole village will have to leave the valley," Marigold said gently. "He can't stay, Dresden. I'm sorry, but it's true."

Dresden's heart sank. How could she turn him away? She loved Rain. He must feel the same way about her, or he wouldn't keep coming back. Life was a dream when she talked with him. Her existence would lose its luster if Rain went away.

Unless...perhaps she went *with* him? An idea flickered to life in her mind. He was a god, after all. Surely, Rain knew of a way they could remain together. How absurd, not to think of it before!

"I will tell him so tomorrow," Dresden promised. Then, because she did care for her friend and felt she owed Marigold the truth, said, "I am going to ask if I can go with him. If he leaves, I will be terribly sad."

"I understand," said Marigold softly, and she left abruptly, returning down the mountain to her village, where people were beginning to think that one's prayers can be answered too much.

Dresden watched her go with a little knot of regret tightening in her dragon's stomach. The next instant, regret soured into anger. It wasn't Dresden's fault if she had changed her mind about staying. Marigold could leave the valley anytime she wanted, really. What was keeping her in the village, if not her own decision?

The next morning, when Rain alighted next to a shivering, smiling Dresden, the she-dragon told him of the villager's troubles. "And that is why I want to ask if I may come with you," she said, "wherever your home is. For I couldn't bear to never see you again. I love you, Rain."

"I feel the same about you," the god answered.

Dresden's heart fluttered and fell, like one of her bright, hot sparks.

"But I am a fire-breather, and you are rain," she said. "How can we be together? Do you know anything that could help us?"

Rain thought for a moment, then his face brightened like a sun-lined cloud. "Yes, I know just the thing. I can turn you into a goddess. There is a magic well in the Cloud Citadel, where I live. If you wish to live as a goddess with me, then I will go and fetch you a drink from this well."

"Oh, yes," Dresden nodded, "I wish it." Then Rain flew away and left her for several hours. She wondered what Cloud Citadel was like and what it would be like to live there as a goddess. What form would she take as an immortal being? How long was forever to one who never died?

He came sweeping back bearing a cup that shone like silver. "If you drink this, it will transform you into a goddess. One cup every day for three days, and then your transformation will be complete. It may hurt," he said softly, stroking her shining, red-scaled cheek. He winced as steam hissed from his hand. "But just as you are a beautiful dragon, you will make a beautiful goddess."

"A little pain won't deter me," Dresden said. Rain remained with her while she took the first gulp. A cold, sharp pain rippled through her body and her bones jostled one another like knives. If she hadn't seated herself, she might have fallen over. The pain made her screw her eyes shut until it abated.

When she opened her eyes, she was looking up at Rain. She was much smaller than before. Her scales had melded together to make a seamless, soft skin, rusty red and gold colored like her scales. Otherwise, she was still a dragon: wings, claws, and jaws.

"Are you well?" Rain asked her.

Dresden nodded.

"I am," she said. Even her voice sounded different.

"The cup will refill itself every day for the next two days," Rain said. "Drink it once more tomorrow. On the third day, I will come and fetch you here at noon. Now, I must leave you and these poor, damp villagers." He embraced her once, wincing only briefly, and then flew away, leaving a trail of misty rain in his wake. Dresden felt an ache that had nothing to do with the contents of the cup. So this was love, she thought, and put the ache down to her partial transformation.

The next morning when she awoke in her cave, she discovered that the cup had indeed refilled itself. She swallowed the contents in one gulp. This time the world spun and a pain shot through her head, filling it with a terrible sound like thunder till she thought it might break her apart.

A shadow darkened the cave entrance. A tall figure stood there, holding a rough bag.

"Dresden?" came Marigold's astonished voice. "What has happened to you?"

The dragon looked down at herself and almost yelped. Her skin was one color, golden brown like Marigold's, and a curtain of brown hair brushed across her—her shoulders! Dresden patted her human shoulders and felt her way to her face. She yelped this time. Instead of a long snout, she felt a short nose, smooth cheeks, and full lips. Holding out her arms, she saw that her hands and feet remained clawed. She spun around and felt a welcome tug at her back. Dresden looked almost fully human, but she retained her wings.

"Oh, Marigold," she said. "Rain brought me a cup from the magic well in his Cloud Citadel, and it is transforming me into a goddess so that I may go and live with him."

Marigold looked very sober. "Is this what you wish for?" she asked. "To change this much?"

"Yes," said Dresden, her voice ringing stranger than ever in her ears.

"Very well," said Marigold. She looked down at the bag in her arms. "I brought you poetry yesterday and today, in case you missed reading."

"I did. I do," Dresden assured her. She noticed for the first time that none of the other girls had come to visit her in a long time, but said nothing about that. They could hardly be blamed for her long absences. "Please stay with me, dear Marigold, if you have the time."

Marigold sat with her legs crossed and looked at the book in her lap. "Dresden," she said, "I've also come to tell you something. I'm leaving tomorrow. To go to a university."

Dresden had no need to ask if this was what Marigold wanted; she had wanted it as long as she had known her. "I'm very happy for you," she said, and she meant it, though the words felt heavy and sharp. "Imagine. We're both getting what we want. Not so out of reach after all."

"No," said Marigold. "I suppose not."

So they sat together and read poetry. Dresden found she could hold the books by herself, though her claws tore the pages once or twice. Marigold wrapped her in her own cloak, for she was very cold and couldn't produce a single spark when she tried.

When at last Marigold had to leave, Dresden begged her to come back tomorrow and say goodbye.

"Of course, I will," the girl answered.

That night Dresden flew higher into the mountains, looking over the sunset-drenched valley and thinking how much had changed since her arrival. No doubt the Cloud Citadel offered many spectacular sights. Still, she would miss this place, and she would miss Marigold even more. Ah, but Marigold was leaving too, going at last to the university where she could study her beloved poetry. Everything was as it should be.

She shivered and clutched the cloak around her. Tearing holes for her wings had been easy, but human skin was so much more tender than scales. That would take some getting used to. Dresden scattered her thoughts like seeds, trying to leave them high up in the sky, and flew home.

The following day, she waited for Marigold to come. Once or twice she almost drank from the full cup. Each time she stopped, telling herself she would say goodbye to Marigold first and then carry it to the stream where she would drink it when Rain arrived. But the girl never appeared.

At last, she could put off leaving no longer. Dresden wrapped herself in the cloak and took the cup, hoping that Marigold would understand. The cloak weighed heavy on her wings as she walked. She didn't much feel like flying, and so left them covered.

The dragon-girl didn't have to wait long for Rain to appear. He came sweeping through the valley as always, and if Dresden's heart didn't soar as it used to, she put it down to the chill.

"My love." The beautiful god stepped to the earth and embraced her without wincing. He stepped back to look at the cup in her hands, keeping his own on her cloaked shoulders. "You waited to drink the last cup? I hoped that you would."

Dresden shivered. Her wings had felt in the way when he hugged her, but now his distance made her feel cold. "Is it cold in the Cloud Citadel?" she asked.

"Not if you don't want it to be. I can make it warm as you like."

Dresden glanced far, far across the valley, the long way Rain had come. "How will I get there?"

"I'll carry you, of course," Rain answered.

Dresden looked at the cup, which she held carefully between herself and Rain. "When I drink this, I will lose my wings."

Rain brushed a strand of hair away from her face. "You won't need them, dearest."

Something strange happened to Dresden. Her chest filled with a painful warmth that had nothing to do with fire. Her face grew wet and she trembled not from cold, but for some other reason. She understood from all the poetry Marigold had read to her that she was sad. Not just sad, but torn and despondent.

"You're crying," said Rain, worry creasing his perfect face. "What is it, Dresden?"

"I was so sure I loved you," she said. Tears poured down her strange, smooth face. "I care for you, I do. I wanted more than anything to go with you. But I cannot give up my wings."

The god's bright eyes turned a sad, pale gray. Slowly, he released her. They faced each other silently for the space of three heartbeats.

"I should never have asked you to be something you are not," he said. He sighed heavily and the trees around them swayed and whispered.

"Farewell, Dresden," Rain said. "You are a beautiful dragon. You would have made a beautiful goddess." He stepped backwards, his eyes trained elsewhere. "Perhaps now is a good time to visit another valley," he murmured. The next instant, he stepped off the cliffside and soared back the way he had come, and thunder rumbled in the distance.

Dresden walked back home feeling limp, heavy, and damp. Only when she came in sight of her cave did she find that she had left the cup by the stream. She didn't feel like going back for it just then.

"Dragon or human?" she murmured, glancing at her small hands with their dull, short nails. "Certainly not goddess." Then she stopped, for there was Marigold climbing up the path she had worn on her many visits, her shoulders drooping beneath the weight of a bulging bag. Her face went pale when she saw Dresden.

"I thought I was too late," the girl said.

Dresden tried to speak, then tried again. "I didn't want to lose my wings," she said. "But I'm not sure if I want to be fully dragon again, or if I even could be."

"Who do you feel like?" Marigold asked.

Dresden thought for a moment. The world looked different, larger. She doubted she would find fresh sheep palatable anymore. But her wings felt the same, though they were smaller; she could still fly as often as she liked. And facing Marigold, Dresden realized she could see a great deal more of the world the way this girl did, and that was better than anything the Cloud Citadel could possibly offer.

She laughed. "I've been a fool," she said. "I feel like myself. Not even a magic cup could change that, really, unless I let it. Still, I wonder if the poets have anything to say about this."

A smile spread across Marigold's lovely face. "Perhaps," she said. "You might also try eating fire berries again, since they strengthened your fire. But I will read with you, if you like."

She made a tiny surprised noise when Dresden hurried forward and embraced her. Marigold's arms rose to return the embrace. Though her arms settled gently over Dresden's cloaked wings, the dragon-girl felt lighter than ever, and all the cold of the past few weeks melted away.

"Will you be there long?" Dresden asked.

She and Marigold stood at the edge of a forest, where shadows hid them from the sprawling city not far away. In the distance, the spires of a large building stood out like a beckoning hand. Marigold turned shining eyes to Dresden.

"I'm not sure," she said. "I don't know how long this will take. But I will visit you as often as I can. Perhaps one day, you could even visit me. If you wish it, of course."

"To see you again?" Dresden smiled and squeezed the girl's hand. "I wish for nothing else."

She watched Marigold leave the shelter of the trees and walk toward the city, feeling a strange swelling in her heart. It was not the sadness she had felt watching Rain disappear, though this, too, she recognized because of the poetry she had read. She felt happy in a tender sort of way. Not just happy, but peaceful, even mended.

"Goodness," she said to herself as she flew home over the vast, green forest, "a dragon in love with a human. I wonder if the poets have anything to say about this."

Some things, she mused, changed one way or another like a sudden gush of cold water. But the things that lasted, no matter how strange or unexpected they were, came quietly and stayed forever, like words printed on a page long ago.

The villagers in Shining Valley have long ceased to pray for rain. They speak often of the summer of the deluge, until the story almost eclipses the story of the dragon. Almost, but not quite.

Every now and then they catch a glimpse of a winged creature gliding among the distant peaks. Some think it is the dragon. Others think it is too small—a large bird of prey, perhaps. The dragon may have left in search of easier feeding grounds. Still, no bird of prey ever carried a human figure, a female figure, clasped to its chest while in flight, as some swear they've seen.

Those who glimpse that sight mutter about dragons carrying off tender maidens, only they don't say anything to one another. The maidens who once may have foolishly wandered up to the dragon's lair have gone about their lives and never speak of *that,* not anymore.

Marigold was the only one who claimed to know anything about dragons. Though a few people wish they had listened to her, they have lost their chance. Marigold left the village long ago. She has gone to study poetry someplace far away, and the villagers haven't seen her for years.

But Dresden still lives in her cave. She has made it more comfortable now that she has no intention of leaving. And of all the residents of Shining Valley, Dresden knows she is the happiest–though whatever form she chose to keep, only she and Marigold can say.

The Witch's Caveat

S pying on me, are we? You have stood there waiting the past hour, not so silent as you think. I gather more than herbs, you see, and the forest keeps little from me. But have no fear. Why the terrified face? What can I do to you? Come out and tell this old woman what it is you want.

Oh, am I the witch? You want an answer, then, and perhaps something more, as others often do. I am indeed *a* witch. But have you not heard? There are tales of several who live in these woods. Old crones like me and young maidens just past their first blush of youth. How do you know I am the one you seek?

You want to hear my story, you say. Are you certain? Another's story is not easily forgotten, no matter whether it incites terror or joy, disgust or pleasure.

You insist. You want to make sure I am the one you seek. Very well then, I agree, and I want something in return. It is a fine summer's day. The forest is warm and sweetly scented, and I am done gathering these herbs. Come, walk with me.

Do you object to going to a witch's house? Some do. The villages here are not all friendly with my kind. Of this, no doubt you are aware. Yet my price is your company on my way home. A story heard is a journey taken, and this story is a long one.

A fair warning on the subject of stories: if you hope for a happy ending, a tale of ease and love and tidy conclusions, you may find yourself disappointed by the end of mine. It begins on my eighteenth birthday.

We were at dinner, my father and I, about to go our separate ways when he informed me that I was to be married. Maël Fontaine had agreed to take my hand in marriage. I remember standing alone in the dim, vast room, thinking this over after he left. On one hand, the announcement was no surprise to me. My father never asked my opinion on anything. Why should my marriage, that institution which is the inevitable end for all women of wealth—for wealthy I once was—be any different?

Yet trained as I had been to expect this departure from home, I wished to learn what I might expect in my new life. Who was this Maël Fontaine, my groom-to-be? At least I had a more forthcoming source of information than my father.

"Oh, he's wealthy enough, Miss Amandine," Cook confided. Cook seemed to gather all the news in the land, sifting it like chaff until she found the wheat. But this was hardly news; my father would settle for nothing less than a wealthy match. Desjardins' roses were the most sought after in all the land, the only ones famed for growing year-round. Both my father's blooms and his name had graced the courts of many a king. No doubt my betrothed possessed wealth, rank, or both. I caught the sidelong glance Cook gave my maid Heloise as she said, "Fearful handsome too, I hear."

"But what is he like?" I pressed.

"I heard he is a great sorcerer." Heloise's eyes widened with the significance of her offering. "Greatly feared in the surrounding villages, miss, and revered by all."

The thought of marrying a sorcerer was intriguing, but the rest did not sit well with me. "Tell me more," I said, but Cook said that was all she knew, and Heloise hurried me back to my room to dress for dinner without another word.

Either the staff had been sworn to secrecy, or my groom-to-be was excessively secretive, for I learned no more of him in the following months. My time at home ended far too swiftly. On a spring morning, I said farewell to Cook and Heloise—a new maid awaited me in my new home—and my father took me to the church, where I met my intended for the first time at the altar.

Maël Fontaine was indeed handsome. He possessed a proud, aristocratic face framed by thick brown hair and sharp green eyes that surveyed my father's legal documents greedily like a predator that stalks its prey. I discovered only then that I was to inherit the entirety of my father's business upon his death.

The first words between Fontaine and I were our wedding vows. The groom leered at me throughout the ceremony. It was over quickly: the priest's droning formalities, two signatures, and my life was yet again someone else's. My father bade me a gruff goodbye, and I never saw him again.

We traveled immediately to my husband's estate, a large mansion in the distant countryside. I remember my first sight of it: sprawling in the dark, surrounded by vast woods so dense I could not make out even the faintest flicker of light from the nearest village. As we approached, lanterns along the drive cast a golden glow, allowing me a clearer sight of the house. It rose some four stories into swooping rooftops and pointed spires, marked here and there with mullioned, gabled windows that seemed to gape at our arrival. Nothing passed those windows unnoticed, I felt. There was no mistaking it. This was an old house, and much care and money had gone into its upkeep. My father had indeed made a shrewd business arrangement.

"See there," said my new husband, "the pride of my life. You will soon enough know the ways of this place."

Now, by all appearances, I had made a fortuitous match; with a wealthy husband and a grand house, I would never lack the comforts to which I was accustomed. Many women have fared worse. But surely you have guessed by now how unhappy I was.

Our married life did little to improve my first impression of my husband. The house was indeed his pride, as was his wealth; he lived as though all he owned gave him the power and authority of a king. Most of Fontaine's time and energy was spent in overseeing its care or hosting elaborate parties where, it seemed, his biggest goal was to display this wealth. I was an accessory. These events tired and bored me. Occasionally, he alarmed me with his gross boasting of conquests monetary and magical, boasting that invested guests smiled at or ignored as if this unpleasantness must be endured.

Guests on business soon learned that the free-flowing wine at these dinners was not their ally. In drunkenness, Fontaine became irascible, even violent. More than one business venture fell through after a night of such behavior. Those were the nights I grew to fear the most. Deprived of the company of his guests, he turned his attention to me. In those times I learned soon enough that crossing him was a costly mistake. Perhaps you will understand why I don't wish to dwell on those early months. I leave them in the past, where they belong.

I did ask him about his business once, before the tipping point. What did it consist of? How did he run it? Could I participate in some way? Perhaps, I thought foolishly, if I could at least work with him, he might come to see me as an equal, a human with a brain and a will, not just something to use or display. But he only laughed and brushed my question aside as if it were a bothersome fly. Sometimes I wondered if Fontaine's true sorcery lay in distancing himself from all human warmth and sympathy. Was there any spark of kindness beneath his handsome, arrogant exterior? I soon ceased to ask that question. His money was real, but I saw no more evidence of his magic than I did of his capacity for kindness. Both titles of sorcerer and husband were nothing more than words to me.

If he refused to grant me access to this world of money and numbers, I at least gained some relief during his business-related absences. Then, even the tense atmosphere among the staff relaxed into timid relief. I, who was used to friendly exchanges with the servants in my father's house, worked to win two or three of them over during these times.

First, there was my own maid, a stolid, dependable woman named Margot. She possessed a good nature hidden beneath her no-nonsense bearing. Then there was patient old Gaspard, the butler, who had served my husband's father before him. He always knew how long my husband would be away; and, unlike my husband, would tell me the time frame. Lastly, there was Gabi, one of the new laundry maids who also sometimes worked in the kitchen. She was gentle and pretty in a pale, frightened way, and I gave her jobs that kept her well out of sight from my husband when he was at home.

The library was my other solace. Not only did I find books on my favorite topics—literature, poetry, and history—but on something else. This new topic piqued my interest more than all the rest: the art of magic. At first I resisted my curiosity out of fear that Fontaine might see my study of this particular art as a threat. But as I mentioned before, as time went on, I never saw him practice magic nor found any indication that he did. My fear that he might feel threatened by my actions proved to be unfounded, almost laughably so. He took only an intermittent interest in me, and I was free to spend most of my time as I chose.

Learning this new art filled my days with more purpose and meaning than I'd ever known. My own aptitude surprised me. I had no idea if my ability to learn magic was due to the magic itself or a family disposition; undoubtedly, my father employed some kind of magic to grow his roses year-round. Whether he performed it himself or hired another, I never knew. I clung to my course of study with the fervor of someone who has found the secret to life itself.

Did you know that some spells take a physical form that can be seen and manipulated only by the spell caster? Others are invisible, sensed only by those attuned to the practice. I quickly learned a number of small spells, ranging from simple charms to incantations for protection. My room became a makeshift spellcraft room, supplied by a grumbling but dutiful Margot with silver bowls of water and other materials. I trusted only myself with the books of magic.

Some might say I stole these books. I never returned them to their shelves, and as a wife is little more than her husband's possession, what right had I to keep them? Ah, but is not marriage also a merger? If I belonged to this household, then I took great care of its objects. In any case, I didn't care if what I did was thievery. The first time I used a spell to keep the sorcerer from my chambers at night, I rejoiced in everything I had taken from him and reclaimed as my own.

From then on, I saw him very little. Occasionally I still had to dine with him and his guests, though his inebriated rages never touched me again. My own magic abilities seemed to dissuade him from attempting anything on me besides snarled threats and drunken curses in the privacy of our own company. Or perhaps I no longer interested him. With winter approaching, I looked forward to long evenings alone, for Fontaine rarely invited friends to dinner and often kept to himself in the cold months. How foolish I was to think this reprieve would last.

One day when I thought he was out overseeing some business, I happened upon him in the morning room. He held a letter, and his face was pale with terrible anger.

"Your father is dead," he said, "and by some great misfortune, blight has ravaged the roses. Half my fortune is destroyed."

The news of my father's death struck me like a blow. I'd written to him not long ago, asking him to tell me how he ran his business. I thought that, with my practice of magic, we might now have something in common. He had never replied. Now I would never know if it was the result of his indifference to me, or if he simply died before he had the opportunity to send an answer.

Fontaine interrupted my thoughts. "This is the sole survivor of this wretched business." He clutched a single crimson rose, holding it out to me like a portent of ruin. Before I could move, he snatched my arm in a claw-like grip. "You have ruined me," he said in a terrible, low voice that struck more fear in me than his rages ever could. And yet, the injustice of being blamed for something I had no part in loosened my tongue.

"I've no more ruined you than you have shown me respect," I said, returning his gaze. "And my father never cared to tell me the inner workings of my own inheritance. But if you tell me about it now, I could help you, and we might salvage it together."

Do you think I should have known better than to appeal to him again? Was I the instigator of both our fates here? And who has the right to judge me, when all I did was use what little power I possessed to protect myself?

You remain silent, listener. The story continues.

He laughed at my words, a cold and detached sound, so different from the explosive anger I was familiar with. Suddenly, I felt weak; something more than fear numbed my brain as his grip on my arm tightened painfully. A strange magic thrummed in the air and pressed against me.

"Salvage," he said, drawing out the word in a snarl so that it sounded like *savage*. "You will indeed help me now, in any way I see fit." And tossing the crumpled rose to the floor, he seized me with both hands and dragged me from the room.

My mind was a tangle of terror, all my spells a knot of rose brambles. I could not separate one from the other. Frantic, my mind and body weakening, I spoke the first words I grasped. Whether they belonged to a single spell or formed a strange conglomeration, I had no idea. They took effect at once.

The sorcerer shrieked and released me, stumbling backwards and clawing at his face. My mind cleared at once, the oppression of his magic banished or broken. The shock and relief flooding my body hardened to exultation and loathing. For as I watched, his handsome features contorted and writhed until the moaning form lying before me was no more than a wretched monster.

He rose. His hairy flanks like an animal's quaked with the effort, his face a distortion of man and beast. He caught sight of me through squinting, tiny eyes. Then his bellowing rattled the house and shook my exultation into panic. Had I created my own death, rather than salvation? As the raging monster came toward me, fear propelled my escape. I burst from the room and into the hall as if the wind carried me on its back.

Yet Fontaine was faster.

Something heavy and bitter pushed me to the floor, like a shard of poisoned stone flung against my back. A ragged cry escaped my lips. The room spun and melted. I could not rise. From behind came the crash of a large form against furniture and a roar of rage.

This time anger tempered confusion. I did not create my own escape simply to succumb to death. I rose from the floor, shaking as if I had been the one transformed, and fled again, all the while expecting the bellowing to overtake and stop me once and for all.

Through a silent house, I ran until I reached the dusty and abandoned upper floors. I neither saw Fontaine nor fell prey to his magic, though I expected him to burst into my hiding place at any minute. Why did he not follow me? Why did he not finish what he began? If he possessed magical skills after all, why was I not dead?

I spent a cold night in the attic, waiting for any sign of the monster or his powers, watching the winter sky darken and pale through one window and scarcely able to ask myself what the next day would bring.

The morning brought nothing but hunger and thirst. After several hours, these most pressing needs drove me to seek sustenance. I employed a small charm to render me invisible and stole downstairs. The mansion was eerily quiet, its silent atmosphere unlike any I had experienced before. The hairs on my arms and neck stood upright. Where was the sorcerer?

Even the kitchen was silent and empty. I managed to gather food and drink without incident until I made my way back upstairs.

Muffled sounds sent a thrill of panic through me, and I pressed myself into a recess. A moment later, Gabi and Margot came into view, and though I relaxed somewhat, their conversation brought me little comfort.

"He must've destroyed her," Gabi said. Her face was towards me, but the spell held. She carried a tray of food, and I could see that her eyes were red with crying. "The poor mistress! Not a sign of her anywhere, and her room untouched. I brought her food just in case, but she isn't there."

"Have done with your crying, girl, and go put that away." Margot's back was to me. Suppressed tears ruffled the edges of her stern voice.

"But where–what do you suppose happened?"

Margot huffed. "I've never seen his magic so strong. There's no telling what he did to her. If she's truly dead, it's a sight better than remaining here, what with the master's threats."

"Shouldn't we go looking–" Gabi began, but the older woman cut her off with a shake of her head.

"No." Margot sniffled and wiped her face with her apron. "Don't go meddling. Do you understand me, Gabrielle? Promise me. I promise you she's better off wherever she is."

I longed to reach out and comfort these good women, but I remained in my hiding place. As Margot swept by I heard her mutter,

"Perhaps she deserved it and perhaps she didn't, but pray to heaven we don't end up like her."

Over the next few weeks, I began my secret life. In one of the many attic rooms, I found musty old curtains in a chest and piled them into a kind of nest between two massive armoires that smelled of mothballs. The one tiny window in that room let in pale, gray light.

I left my hiding place every few days only to seek out food. I took very little. I heard whisperings among the servants: the master had shut himself up, the master raged, the master pored over magic books and sought revenge on the spirit of his dead wife. Though I was by all accounts severed from Fontaine, his current state was my fault, and this drove him to pursue me even into the afterlife. This knowledge filled me with dread. The memory of his magic weighing me down, turning my own thoughts to smoke, made me shiver.

Why did I not simply leave, you ask? Well, there were a few reasons. At the time, I believed I was simply too weary from my flight and the magic exerted upon me to leave the mansion. I learned later that the cold also weakened my powers. Developed in summer, my magic waxes and wanes with the year, and it took some time to understand and adapt to this.

But even if that were not the case, where could I have gone, in the depths of winter? The villagers feared the sorcerer, and me by extension. I had no other home.

It was a very poor existence. As you might imagine, I alternated between worry for and anger towards my friends, particularly Margot. Her last words made me wonder if I had overestimated their regard for me. Or perhaps it was fear for her own life that made her speak so. I resolved to keep away from them for their own sake as well as mine.

I missed my books, which I dared not retrieve. Among the dusty rafters and broken furniture, I might have withered into nothing more than a scant knowledge of magic had I remained undiscovered.

One morning, after a night of tossing and turning which kept me up into the gray dawn, I awoke to footsteps tramping softly across the dusty floors. My heart shot into my throat. But before I could perform any spell, Gaspard and Margot appeared around one of the ancient armoires.

Margot shrieked. I rushed forward, arms outstretched, trying to silence her, trying to tell them I was no specter.

A few words assured them that I was indeed alive. In turn, they assured me that the servants, while frightened by the sorcerer's appearance, had suffered no worse from his behavior than they had when he was a man.

"I told you he couldn't have killed her," Gaspard said to Margot, his wrinkled face beaming with smug relief. "Blasted her into oblivion? Impossible, you see, even for him. Nothing but bragging."

But Margot turned mournful eyes to me.

"Oh, mistress," she said, "what have you done?" Her voice carried sadness, reproach, and pity.

"Only what I had to," I assured her, allowing myself to feel nettled. "I've kept away all these weeks to protect you. I heard the sorcerer seeks revenge on me, even though he thought I died. Where else could I go?"

"He's given up on revenge, my lady," Gaspard said. "He never speaks of you now. He's cast off or destroyed the magic books in his rooms. His only desire is to return to his former shape."

I laughed bitterly. So soon? Even the act of turning him into a monster could not make him remember me for long. That offered me some tentative relief. But even if I knew how to undo my spell, I vowed I never would.

Aloud, I admitted, "I'm not even sure what kind of spell I have put on him, nor how to remove it." I exhaled suddenly and sat back down on my nest. Even speaking about the event wearied me.

Gaspard cleared his throat. "Off with you, Margot, and bring Lady Amandine some food," he commanded.

Despite the maid's initial misgivings, she and Gaspard not only kept my location secret, but brought me food and a few other necessities. To my great relief, Fontaine hadn't touched the books of magic in my room, and these Margot brought to me. I stayed in the attic throughout the long and weary winter, and there I resumed my studies.

The more I learned, the more I understood how small my grasp of magic was. In the debilitating chill, I read about herblore and other crafts of nature I'd never studied before. Plants have the ability to heal bruises and lacerations, and not just of the body, but sometimes of the heart as well. Perhaps I could find a cure for my own uneasy heart, wounded as it was from a life of neglect and abuse from those I'd hoped would offer compassion and companionship. But herblore was not some idea to study in a book; I needed to go out and let nature teach me herself.

I would often gaze out the window, dreaming of spring and a life beyond these secret chambers, and then I would remember why I was trapped. Not only did the cold weaken my powers, but I feared Fontaine's. I could not leave without expending considerable energy, and I worried that doing so would alert the one I had disfigured.

My friends brought me news of him, too. The sorcerer kept to his own chambers and admitted no visitors. He tried, they said, to return to his former state through his own magic. The results were almost as fearful as the spell I had cast upon him, for he only succeeded in inflicting boils and festering, pus-filled wounds on himself. And I felt certain that, try as he might, he could never return to his former state. Had I not given him his true form? The thought offered me a bitter comfort.

One blessed morning, after the first signs of spring appeared on the trees and the snow had all but melted, I made my way outside at last. The warmth and my invisibility charm lent me the strength and courage to wander out every day. I breathed in the fresh air like a healing vapor.

Soon, further armed with Gaspard's information, I marked the boundaries of the estate and set out into the forest beyond. Happy were the hours I spent deep in the woods, knowing I walked in the wild, beyond any place the sorcerer had ever set foot. The more time I spent there, the more the woods and I became acquainted, and at last I began to practice the branches of magic I had only read about.

Disguised as an old woman, I went into the villages to purchase some essentials. I bought small items such as a mortar and pestle, a set of small knives for cutting and parsing herbs, silver and wooden bowls for scrying, and flint for starting my own fires. If I was to practice magic, it would be with my own tools.

Magic was forbidden in most villages. While my careful purchases were viewed as the eccentric preferences of an old woman, I overheard more than one young maid receive a scolding for voicing any curiosity regarding either magic or the secretive and powerful sorcerer in the woods, both of which were far removed from their simple lives.

Colorful and varied tales of Fontaine's ill luck spread among the villagers. Some said he had been cursed by a jealous sorcerer. No, others said, his wife had killed him out of spite, or for his money. Oh no, he still lived, said housewives with wistful eyes, the wife was without a jot of magic herself. And why would she want to harm such a handsome husband?

Often the injustice and stupidity of these tales made me tremble with anger. But in a way they protected me, too. No one would venture onto the sorcerer's grounds unless they had business there. And I knew that old Gaspard would turn anyone away before they could see the sorcerer, more for their own protection than his masters'.

One day, just beyond one corner of the sorcerer's grounds, I found a derelict shack in a forest clearing. It was sturdy, despite its neglect. I stored my small supply of tools here, visiting it every day to clean and repair it. Soon it became my favorite place to practice herblore and to read the stars at night.

In my studies, I learned more about what I had done to the sorcerer. I had changed not just his form, but his destiny: my spell eternally denied him the release of death. This revelation began to trouble me. It was not, as you may suppose, my conscience that felt uneasy. I felt no guilt for defending myself. I had meant to make him suffer– yes, that too, as he had made me suffer–and for that I felt no guilt either.

But sometimes at night, as I lay trying to sleep in the attic, it felt as if the spell itself tugged at me, leaving me with some undefinable ache, a deep splinter in my soul connected to his very existence. Whatever he had tried to do to me just before I transformed him had failed. I remembered that terrible throb of magic. Always on the alert for it, I never once sensed that oppressive power anywhere in the mansion. Still, Fontaine never spoke of me or sought revenge. For all I knew, I truly had ceased to exist for him. But he troubled me still. Something bound us together, something I could not escape by remaining in my prisoner's house.

By this time, I had transformed the shack into a cottage. With the help of my friends, I transferred essentials there piecemeal. I brought the books of magic. Margot surprised me by bringing some finer things from my grand and abandoned bedroom: a small, thick rug, a bundle of unused candles, a well-used but sturdy cloak among sumptuous gowns.

"They're yours, my lady," she said. "No one else has any use for them."

I accepted everything gratefully, save for my fine gowns. I had no use for them anymore.

We spent an evening setting up the place. When I had said goodbye to my friends, I looked around at my new home and finally understood that I had left the grounds and my prison behind forever.

The cottage was a snug, one-room affair. A rough stone fireplace dominated one wall, over which a polished beam of wood served as a shelf. A thin pallet lay near another wall. I scarcely had room for two salvaged chairs. Gaspard himself repaired a large shelf on one wall that served as dining and work table. My bunches of herbs and edible roots hung from the rafters, and beneath the corner windows, I stored my implements in a cupboard. The porch covering, now repaired with fresh thatch, shielded my outdoor work area from some of the elements. The nearby stream served as my water source.

It was by far the most humble of dwellings I had ever known, and yet I loved it because it was mine. It was my pride and joy. (You will see it soon.) I learned how to forage and cook my own food, meager fare though it was. This place allowed me to live on my own terms.

But even a home of my own could not ease my ache or calm my uneasiness. Despite my growing knowledge and practice of magic, I had found nothing in plants, stars, or books that could sever the cord tying me to the monster. After a few weeks, I reached a conclusion.

Living far from the mansion was not enough. As long as Fontaine lived, I could never truly be free. I had but one choice.

One fair summer's night, I cloaked myself in the invisibility charm and crept into the sorcerer's chambers. My limbs trembled at the sight of the hulking form on the bed. There he slept, a ragged, stinking mountain of matted filth and hair, his face twisted even in sleep. Loathing granted no space for pity. I was not the only one tied to his fate. With his death, I would be granting my friends their freedom as well as mine.

The spell's image hung above his head, just visible in the faint moonlight. I reached for it when an unpleasant thought gave me pause.

Could I really take another's life? I despised him, but I had never killed anything, and the thought brought bile up into my throat. His death would end his suffering, but could I live with myself as a murderer? Cold reason whispered that it would be a crueler punishment to let him suffer for eternity. Let him remain marked by my choice as I had been controlled by his. I withdrew my hand from the spell and let its image fade.

Yet my purpose returned to me. If he lived, would I ever be free?

Oh, I was at war with myself: let him suffer, and be tied to him forever; kill him and destroy this bond, but stain my hands with another's blood. I touched the spell and examined it, searching all its angles for some clue, some way I could break it. I could find none. I froze when he turned in his sleep and groaned.

It was a sound I knew well: one of deepest, unseen misery. I gritted my teeth as another, even more unwelcome thought came to me: perhaps in this form, had he shown me kindness, I could have loved him as I never could have loved him in his proud and cruel human shape. I shook my head. An absurd thought, I told myself. And anyway, the chance for that was long past.

I could not undo the spell, nor did I wish to. Neither could I live with myself if I murdered him, no matter how much I despised him. I had to find a third way.

And then all at once, I knew what to do.

The spell glowed in my hands as I found the tiniest opening at one angle. There I set a caveat: a condition that, if met, would allow the spell to break and free me from him forever. Perhaps I changed nothing, I thought, for the caveat involved something as unlikely to happen as snow in summer. But I had no other ideas. At least my actions subdued the warring parts within me for now. The effort had exhausted my strength. I left the spell and the monster and made my way back home.

That summer was a golden one, a blessedly long season that enabled me to continue my work with joy. Gabi and Margot came to see me at the cottage now and then. Even Gaspard joined them occasionally, despite complaining of his arthritis, and I would whisper a secret spell to ease the pain in his joints.

Their company brought me welcome solace. Just as importantly, they assured me that the sorcerer kept to himself. All three of them looked peaceful and content. This set me at a tremulous ease for their sake, and made me even more certain I had made the right decision to live alone in the woods. We shared herbal teas and news from the village in our seclusion, tucked away from prying eyes and wagging tongues.

Or so I thought. If the villagers nearby were against one of their own performing magic, they seemed to have no qualms about seeking a witch's aid. To my initial alarm, word spread of the old witch who had taken up residence at the heart of the forest. People from villages on the other side of the forest began to seek me out as well. It was only one or two every week at first, then one or two a day, sometimes more. We traded spells for items I needed. While I relaxed over time and began to enjoy the work and the interactions, people always came with pleading, furtive eyes and mumbled requests: something for a sore that refused to heal, something for sleepless nights, a soothing spell to calm a troubled mind.

Those last requests were the most difficult to fulfill. I might offer a mix of herbs with a blessing, but if anything worked on those with uneasy souls, it was less magic and more the relief gained from a sympathetic listener. I had yet to discover a charm that might offer me true peace of mind.

Though I'd never lived with more purpose than I did now, trouble visited me at night and kept me from sleep. By candlelight, I searched for spells to ease the ache, another way to free myself in the likelihood that my caveat never worked. It was such a small one, after all.

There had to be something in the vastness of magic that could help me. I searched the stars for wisdom but could find nothing to help. During the day, buried in my work, I could convince myself that in time all would be well. All would be well, all would be well; I repeated the words like a charm, but every nightfall, I admitted I had little faith in them.

As winter approached, I began preparing for the cold, remembering how sluggish and dreary the last one had left me. I was on my way back from collecting wood one late autumn day when I came upon the unconscious girl.

She was thinly clad, all but frozen. Her loose auburn hair spilled across the frosty earth. The burn on her arm marked her as an outcast. Her village must have punished her for trying to practice the magic arts and abandoned her here to die. With a shock like snow on skin, I realized she was scarcely younger than I, though I wore my crone's disguise. Had she left behind a sweetheart? Did anyone at home think of her with grief, or had she, too, been discarded without a backward glance?

I took her to my home and cared for her. Early the next morning, Margot visited the cottage, bringing welcome provisions.

She appraised the newcomer, tutting under her breath. "The poor thing. She looks like a scarecrow. I'd have brought more if I knew you had a guest." Margot's description was accurate. The sleeping girl had spent a feverish night, tossing and twisting the bedsheets. Now that the trial had passed, she looked paler and more gaunt than ever.

My guest awoke that afternoon as I worked at my table. Moon-dark eyes scrutinized me in silence.

"Can you tell me your name?" I asked.

"My name?" She said it like a question, one she had forgotten the answer to. She had the kind of voice men like, I am told, high and soft, unlike mine. She turned her face to the ceiling, bitterness on every feature. "I wanted more. They took everything." She closed her eyes in an expression of weariness I well remembered.

"Rest," I told her, and gave her a bowl of soup. "Tell me later."

She spoke when I had turned away. "I want to learn magic. I have some skill, you know. They punished me for that."

"I could teach you," I offered.

She seemed to consider this. After a few moments' silence, I went back to my concoctions.

"Is there a sorcerer in these woods?"

The question put me on my guard. "Yes," I said slowly, my back to her as I worked. "But he sees no one."

"Perhaps no one was insistent enough."

"Do not go looking for things better left alone," I urged, but when I turned, the girl was looking about the one room with its simple, rough furnishings. She fixed me with her moon-dark eyes.

"I've already lost everything," she said, and went back to her soup.

There was something furtive about my guest. She spoke little the rest of that day, answering my questions so briefly that I soon ceased to ask them. Her silence piqued my curiosity. Despite her leanness, she was a hardy girl to have survived what she did, no doubt strengthened by her own determination. It was a determination I underestimated.

I never knew what skills she possessed or what she did to me, but I slept deeply that night. In the morning, I awoke to an empty cottage. The air smelled of snow and the sky was iron gray; the girl wore only her thin clothes and the shawl I'd given her, and her strength would not save her from a winter storm. I hurried out and created a simple spell to track her. I did not bother with my crone's disguise now. Time was of the essence.

The first flakes of snow began to fall just as the spell told me where she had gone. A double chill showered me. My visitor sought the mansion.

I couldn't send a spell to warn anyone. I had never communicated with them by magic for fear that such a strong spell might alert the sorcerer to my presence. I pressed ahead in the thickening snow until a storm whirled around me and weakened the tracking spell. The cold hindered my magic and my progress. If I stayed out much longer, I would lose more than my way home.

I had turned back when the faintest signal reached me, throbbed, and disappeared. The girl had found her destination. There was nothing else I could do; the cold gripped my bones and numbed my mind, forcing me home. I could only hope that Gabi, Margot, or Gaspard would find her and keep her from harm.

The blizzard's chill laid me low for a month. I slowly regained my health, tucked away in a world of glittering, blinding white. My cottage was snug as a badger's burrow and my mind almost as blank as the world outside.

My strength returned slowly. I picked up my studies and practice again, but with this vigor came my familiar uneasiness. I still did not sleep well. Sometimes when I fell into slumber, I dreamt of cramped rooms too small to stand up in, and my ache settled inexplicably in my leg; when I looked down, I saw a string tied my ankle, and at the end of it, a creature skulked in the shadows. It yanked on the string and I fell, dragged toward the lurking terror, and I saw the rageful face of the monster I had made. Screaming, I awoke in my cottage. I breathed in the bitter fragrance of dried herbs until they calmed me, but sleep never returned on those nights.

Without my friends' and visitors' occasional company, I grew lonely. Still I pressed on; there is much to learn when the earth is cold. In my cottage, the natural world was closer to me than it had been in the attic, and I was eager to overcome my weakness to the cold as much as possible so that I might continue my search for freedom.

One morning, to my delight, Gabi appeared at my door, bringing her welcome presence and troubling news.

"The girl you sent, Elise," she said. "She is a great help to us. She seems eager to repay your kindness by assisting your friends."

This puzzled me on several counts. "I did not send her, but I am glad she is helpful. But I fear for her, and for all of you, if she crosses paths with the sorcerer. Is she not afraid of him?"

"Not at all. She's set herself to work, bold as anything. She seems to have a little magic of her own. Oh, nothing so strong as yours. Even though the master stirs from his rooms now and then, she just laughs off our warnings. Even Margot's not sure whether to scold or admire her."

Alarm jangled in my brain. "Stirring? Where does he go?" And why? If he left his lair now, even occasionally, no wonder I had slept so poorly of late. I feared Gabi and the others— especially this bold Elise, whom I did not trust—might be in more danger than they knew. Might this story of repaying my kindness be a cloak for something else?

But Gabi seemed unconcerned. "He only paces the floor of the mansion outside his rooms. Once or twice I thought I saw him in the gardens, but that was weeks ago. He always avoids us on these excursions. I saw him myself only once." A hint of uncertainty flashed across her pale, pretty face. "He must have heard me, for he stopped and looked in my direction. But he only lumbered away."

At this, I began searching my shelves for a message-carrier. Muttering a few words over a single blue-tipped feather, it fluttered briefly in my palm, then stilled as the magic settled on it. I pressed it into Gabi's hand. "If anything happens, speak my name over this," I said. "It will tell me to come to the mansion."

She must have caught something in my expression, for she turned and gave my arm a squeeze. "Have no fear for us," she said. "As for Elise, perhaps she only needs time to prove herself."

"I worry she will prove to be more trouble than she is worth," I said.

Gabi shrugged. "If a wealthy lady can become a powerful witch, perhaps a village outcast can become a wise lady."

I watched Gabi leave through the white and brown woods. If something happened to my friends, it would hardly matter if my magic alerted the sorcerer to my presence. Perhaps she was right about Elise. But Gabi was young; she had seen even less of the world than I.

A few brave souls came to me for aid as winter reached its end. By now, some had seen me both with and without my crone's disguise. They never spoke of this discrepancy, no doubt fearing to mention it and putting it down to a witch's eccentricities. And the world is full of woods, who is to say how many of us there are, practicing in the depths of the forest?

These requests kept me busy, for which I was grateful. And then the message-carrier arrived one gray dawn in spring.

It fluttered through the window, fizzing and sparking, sending jolts of magic down my limbs and fear knocking on my heart. There was no time to lose. I hurried to the mansion at once.

The unfurling spring morning seemed at odds with my haste. The ground was all new grass and slogging mud. The spell led me to the gardens. Beyond the garden wall lay a wide stone staircase leading to the flower beds. As I climbed the steps, the acrid reek of broken magic assaulted me. The sight of two disheveled forms lying on the grass stopped me in my tracks.

I recognized the auburn-haired girl and the brown-haired man. They lay across the central garden path as if a great force had flung them apart. They stirred and sat up, then sought each other. Sunlight poured around me and lit their startled, eager faces.

I must have moved, for they registered my presence then, and fear dawned on their faces. The girl cried out in alarm. The sorcerer threw his arms out to shield her and turned to me.

"Don't hurt us," he begged, his voice shaking. "Don't hurt her. She's done nothing wrong." It was a desperate, pathetic plea.

Did he not recognize me? No, not at first. I watched as fear and recognition dawned in his eyes. A moment later, he pressed himself facedown and uttered a single word, muffled against the pebbled path: *Mercy.*

This sorcerer, once so proud and selfish, now trembled with the same fear I had known as his wife, cowering before me as though I held his life in my hands. And indeed, I did hold his life in my hands. A broken spell of that magnitude did not leave without also taking some energy from the enspelled. I had become powerful; he was now weak. And he was begging me for mercy.

Should I give it to him, when he had never offered it to me?

Another choice, another thread. Another way to be tied to him or not. I was weary of it all.

And yet...if I chose to deny him mercy, I was not so different from him at his worst. And I understood that this man, as much wrong as he had caused, was just as human as I, and we both knew what it was to be bound by choices we could not control or alter.

As the sky brightened all around us, something lifted from my shoulders, slowly at first. I, not he, held the string that bound us. I would choose mercy's release. I would find my own freedom. I saw that it would not be an easy or smooth road, and yet I felt in that moment more powerful than magic had ever made me.

"Have no fear," I said to them, just as I said to you not long ago when we met. I laughed there in the garden at the strange reversal. Have no fear! No evil tied me to him and no monster ensnared me. My humble caveat had worked. He would never harm me again. "The spell is no more. You both shall have what you desire," I said. And because I felt lighter than I had in a long time, perhaps ever in my life, I skipped back down the steps and ran to my cottage, laughing this time for joy.

After the wedding, my friends came and told me of the new mistress. The girl Elise's secret motives became clear soon enough: she cared little whether he was monster or man, loving only his silver and gold–and, it may be suspected, his sorcery. The sorcerer, however, was as devoted to her as a dog.

"She'll spend his fortune in a year's time," said Gaspard, and we all chuckled, sipping our blackberry wine on a clear summer's eve not unlike this one, now many years ago. We could not help our laughter, but it lacked any real scorn.

Are you disappointed, then? You look uncertain. What is it that troubles you?

You have listened to my long tale, and now here, my cottage comes into view. I have fulfilled your request. What more do you want?

Ah, you want to know about my caveat? Very well. I thought you might.

This is how I altered the spell: the sorcerer needed only to show kindness to one person, humble or great, ugly or beautiful, for the spell to release him at once. I suppose that a wealthy man in a fine house would easily confuse grand gestures with humble demonstrations and declarations of love with simple kindness. He would not be the first man to confuse romantic attachment with genuine regard for another.

By all accounts, they have made a fortuitous match, the besotted sorcerer and his pretty wife. Perhaps they will learn true compassion and generosity as their wealth recedes. Perhaps they will find affection even as the passing of years steals beauty and youth.

My ending? My tale goes on, as does yours. I am content in my cottage. The ache of the past troubles me little and infrequently. I sleep well at night. I welcome my friends often, practice my arts, and make my own way in the world.

So return to your lovely wife and your grand mansion. Make your own better and wiser choices. You may yet win her heart. Who can say what is possible? I am indeed the witch you sought this afternoon, but you must go back and write yourself a new story. You have heard my tale, and in doing so, closed that chapter between us. The charade is played out. There is nothing more for you here.

As for me, this life is better than any romance, for it is real, it is my own, and I am its author.

THE END

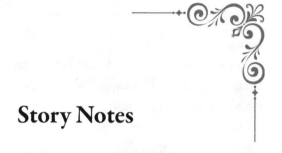

Story Notes

Little Red

I've always been intrigued by stories that turn a narrative on its head somehow. Combining stories is even better! In this case, The Queen of Hearts might not be the megalomaniac we remember from Alice in Wonderland. I also love stories that ask questions. Who's telling the story here? And how does Granny Red pass down her legacy to her granddaughter? I also can't help but wonder about the people of Wonderland. This story has a pretty tight focus, but the implications are broader than what ends up on the page.

Flower Heart

I thought that, since fairy tales often feature shapeshifters and characters who look different, it would be interesting to write a story about someone whose difference in form wasn't outward or visible but was viewed as a threat nonetheless. These stories have the potential to explore what it means to be different and ostracized. Therefore, they can also be a vehicle for exploring what it means to find acceptance. I wrote this story with these things in mind.

Tyrant

Snow White was never my favorite fairy tale, but a series of Instagram posts and prompts stoked a new curiosity in me. (Shout out to Carterhaugh School. Google them if you love fairy tales, folklore, and the art of making meaning.) Why do we pit (step)mothers against daughters? What's really going on with this mirror? Vanora's questions are inspired by these prompts.

This story is begging me to make it a novel. I love that idea, but it's going to have to get in line and wait with the others.

The Dragon of Shining Valley

Another shape-shifter story. But then, these tales are about identity, after all.

This story is based on a prompt taken from Eva Deverell's wonderful blog. (Google her if you love writing and light academia.) I jotted about a third of it down one day, as an exercise in my local writers' group. "Finish me, there's something here!" it demanded. Distant beauty can inspire us to a kind of love, but it can also blind us to the kind of deeper, truer love that comes alongside us softly.

The Witch's Caveat

I love Beauty and the Beast stories. I could write a dozen different versions—maybe I will one day.

The cause or reason for the Beast's curse has always fascinated me, especially since some of the earliest versions of the fairy tale offer little to no explanation for it. Unlike Disney's enchantress, these early tales feature a grand lady or fairy whose role is more ambiguous. Still, the curse drives the story just as much as the patriarchal society that demands wives in exchange for goods or wealth. And while I adore romance, I enjoyed creating a non-romantic ending for Amandine. There's something satisfying about challenging the notion that romantic love is the epitome of happiness for everyone, when in fact there are so many ways of making a good life.

Thank You

I'd like to thank Caitlin, RaeAnne, Indigo, and Hannah for reading these stories and offering such helpful feedback. You are the kindest, most thoughtful critique partners. I'm grateful for your insights that made the stories stronger and for your gentleness that made them easy to receive.

Thank you to Heather, Stephanie, and Dawn for reading earlier versions of some of these stories. There's nothing like enthusiastic friends who can see the potential in rough drafts.

Thank you to Lavender Prose Editing for your editing services and cheerful, positive presence.

Thank you to everyone who helped spread the word, left an early review, and just generally cheered me on. You're the best.

Thank you especially to Mike for reading my stories even when you're tired of looking at words. Hopefully doing so was more fun than researching otitis media. Thank you for your unflagging support. You're the Gryffudd to my Mabyn.

About the Author

Stephanie Ascough lives in sunny Florida, where winters are mild and the heat drains her energy (the opposite of Amandine's experience). She has published one upper middle-grade fantasy, *A Land of Light and Shadow*, and is working on multiple projects at once. When she isn't parenting or feigning housework, she is exploring all things Celtic, fairy tale and folklore related, reading, or playing guitar or mandolin (very poorly but with great enthusiasm). You can sign up for her newsletter[1], find her on Instagram[2], or browse her oft-neglected blog[3].

---

1. https://mailchi.mp/7e678546a5ce/stephanieascoughsnewslettersignup

2. https://www.instagram.com/author.stephanieascough/

3. http://stephanieascough.wordpress.com/